The game had gone too far!

"Not quite as repressed as I'd imagined," he said on an odd note. "Why the withdrawal? You wanted that kiss as much as I did."

"I was taken by surprise..." she began, and let the words trail away as she saw his slow smile.

"That's what they call putting the cart before the horse."

"Stop it!" Her voice had a shake in it. "If you're feeling deprived, you're at liberty to drop me off and go back to your current lady love. Only, don't imagine you're going to use me as a stand-in!"

The smile vanished, giving way to a sudden and dangerous tautening of the jawline. When he spoke, there was no trace of humor left. "If that was the intention, I'd have waited until we were outside your bedroom door before making a move. Is it me you don't trust, or yourself?"

KAY THORPE, an English author, has always been able to spin a good yarn. In fact, her teachers said she was the best storyteller in the school—particularly with excuses for being late! Kay then explored a few unsatisfactory career paths before giving rein to her imagination and hitting the jackpot with her first romance novel. After a roundabout route, she'd found her niche at last. The author is married with one son.

Books by Kay Thorpe

HARLEQUIN PRESENTS
1261—SKIN DEEP
1301—STEEL TIGER
1356—AGAINST ALL ODDS
1397—INTIMATE DECEPTION
1446—NIGHT OF ERROR
1501—TROUBLE ON TOUR

HARLEQUIN ROMANCE
2151—TIMBER BOSS
2232—THE WILDERNESS TRAIL
2234—FULL CIRCLE

Don't miss any of our special offers. Write to us at the following address for information on our newest releases.

Harlequin Reader Service
P.O. Box 1397, Buffalo, NY 14240
Canadian address: P.O. Box 603,
Fort Erie, Ont. L2A 5X3

KAY THORPE

Lasting Legacy

Harlequin Books

TORONTO • NEW YORK • LONDON
AMSTERDAM • PARIS • SYDNEY • HAMBURG
STOCKHOLM • ATHENS • TOKYO • MILAN
MADRID • WARSAW • BUDAPEST • AUCKLAND

Harlequin Presents first edition February 1993
ISBN 0-373-11534-2

Original hardcover edition published in 1991
by Mills & Boon Limited

LASTING LEGACY

CHAPTER ONE

TWENTY-FIVE! Gina sat up straighter in her chair as the words penetrated. That was two years away! She needed the money now if she was to carry out the plans she had made on learning of her inheritance.

She could feel Nick Calway's eyes on her, but she refused to glance in his direction. Trustee indeed! In no more than the mid-thirties, he was scarcely old enough to be put in charge of her immediate future this way.

Meeting him yesterday for the first time, her initial impression had been of a man totally in command of himself—an impression confirmed during the course of the day when he had shown little outward sign of sorrow over the loss of his partner. Not that she had known the latter all that well herself. In the past fifteen years, she had seen him at the most a couple of dozen times.

Her father's death at the age of forty-three had brought a pang nevertheless. With her mother so recently remarried, and now living overseas, it had been a double loss. Impossible, of course, to begrudge the happiness her mother had found after so many years on her own. It was wonderful for two middle-aged people to fall in love the way she and Robert had done.

That her own relationship with Paul Milton wasn't quite so head-in-the-clouds made it no less congruent, of course. The fact that he'd chosen her out of all the others he could have had was no small factor. Paul had everything a girl could want in a man: film-star looks, good job, excellent prospects. What more could she ask?

None of which was germane at the moment. Nick Calway didn't strike her as a man who might be easily swayed when it came to carrying out the duties imposed by her father's will, but he might be prepared to see the sense in her proposal. She knew nothing of the business in which he was involved, nor did she want to learn. Physical fitness was her interest, with the setting-up of her own club premises the ultimate aim. She had the financial detail already worked out, and viably, so he could hardly accuse her of lacking planning and forethought.

Having stated the facts, the elderly solicitor was obviously impatient to conclude the meeting. There were necessary formalities to be completed with regard to proving the will, he had said earlier, but that was his job and would call for their attention only at a later date.

'I'm sorry to cut this so short,' he apologised now, 'but I have another appointment in five minutes. You'll both be contacted in a week or two when I have the papers to hand. Until then, there really isn't anything more to be done.'

Nick Calway was first on his feet. 'In that case, we'll say good morning.'

Gina rose too. There was little point in lingering, she had to agree. Any appeal must be made to this man her father had seen fit to put in charge of her finances for the next two years. Langhill was re-putedly one of the most successful time-share developments in the country. Setting her up in her chosen career would surely be no major drain on resources. In all probability it would prove a relief that she wanted no part in the running of the business.

Emerging into the May sunshine, Gina took an appreciative glance at the view of Stirling castle outlined against a pure blue sky, with the distant mountains as a fitting backdrop. The scenery up here was very different from the gentle landscapes of Cambridgeshire. Not as rugged, perhaps, as the Highlands, but dramatic enough for her taste. Under other circumstances, she might have enjoyed spending some time in this part of the world. Prior to this, the farthest north she had ever ventured was Stratford.

'Coffee?' suggested Nick Calway matter of factly. 'We have things to discuss.'

Outwardly collected, Gina shrugged assent and fell into step at his side. His height and athletic build in the pale grey suit made her feel almost petite, despite the fact that she was slightly above average height herself. She was aware of the easy co-ordination in his movements, of the length of stride and spring of step. Honed to a fine edge of fitness and vital with health would be her professional summing up. Certainly no slouch in the macho male stakes. He exuded virility from every pore.

She had seen too many well-kept male bodies at the health club where she worked at present to take more than a passing interest in this one. Their association was one of finance rather than fitness. In her estimation, his type would appreciate the cards-on-the-table approach, so the sooner she got down to laying them out the better. A cup of coffee would help her over the first few awkward moments.

He took her to a nearby public house. Beer and spirits were only a part of the fare on offer these days, Gina reflected, taking a seat in one of the carved alcoves beneath a loaded delft rack while Nick went to order the coffee.

One of the overhead bar lights brought out a faint reddish cast in his thick, teak-brown hair, outlining a profile seemingly hewn from solid granite. That mouth and jawline had never known compromise, came the suddenly depressing thought. It didn't bode too well for what she was to ask.

He brought the cups with him on return. Seated on the opposite curve of the alcove, he rested an elbow along the table edge to survey her with measured calm.

'So?' he invited.

Gina lifted supple shoulders in another brief shrug. 'I can't pretend to be delighted at the way things have turned out. Finding oneself under the control of a total stranger is hardly scheduled to be anything but a shock. If I were still in my teens I could accept it, but I'm more than capable of handling my own affairs.'

'As he hardly knew you, Martin couldn't be sure of that,' came the dry response. 'Believe me, it's a responsibility I could well do without. Finding myself named as trustee came as something of a shock to me too.'

'In which case, you'll probably be glad to have at least some of the problem removed,' she returned, taking the bull firmly by the horns. 'I have a proposition to put to you.'

One dark eyebrow lifted. 'Is that a fact?'

'Not yet,' she said smoothly, 'but I think it might be. I want to open my own health club in Barchester. I've been running aerobics classes for the last three years, and I hold the necessary qualifications in general keep-fit. I have the premises already picked out, and figures available to prove the viability. All I need is the capital.'

There was no telling anything from the steel-grey eyes, which continued to regard her with the same unwavering assessment. 'Did you try the banks?'

Warmth ran up under her skin; she could only hope it hadn't affected her colour. 'Yes, but——'

'No takers.' It was a statement not a question. 'Not *such* an obviously viable proposition, then.'

'The banks,' she said, 'are still reluctant to loan money to a woman, no matter how good the deal. Not that I've tried them all, as yet.'

'Having learned you were to inherit your father's half of the business, you decided to hold your horses.' He sounded cynical. 'Even if Martin hadn't tied things up the way he did, you wouldn't have been able to get your hands on any money until probate was granted.'

Gina bit back the sarcastic retort. This was no time to be taking umbrage over the implied slur on her intelligence. 'I realised that, of course,' she came back coolly. 'I was quite prepared to wait. Naturally, I still am.'

'On the premise that I'll see fit to advance you the capital you need?' He shook his head. 'No go.'

'You haven't even see my figures yet,' she protested. 'The very least you can do is give me a chance to——'

'The very least I can do is carry out your father's last wishes,' he broke in shortly. 'And those didn't include setting you up in a business already over-subscribed.'

'Not in Barchester. That's the whole point. I have a whole list of people prepared to become members if and when.'

'Then they'll be waiting a long time. If you're still of the same mind in two years' time, I might be prepared to buy you out, but in the meantime the answer is a definite no.' He indicated the cup in front of her with a jerk of his head. 'Better get your coffee before it goes cold.'

'Damn the coffee!' she said forcibly. 'This is important! You said you could do without the responsibility.'

'I could do without a whole lot of things,' he returned on a measured note. 'Try exercising a little self-control.'

Gina bit her lip. That the rebuke had been merited made it no less easy to take. It was only at Paul's instigation that she was doing this at all. If it was her father's way of trying to make up for the years of neglect, he had said, why should she feel guilty about taking advantage?

'I don't normally fly off the handle so easily,' she proffered by way of semi-apology. 'It's just that I had such hopes.'

'More than you had feeling for the man who died last week, for sure,' he returned hardily. 'In three years you never once even attempted to come and visit him. And don't try to make out he never asked you, because I know different.'

Head lowered, she said, 'Do you think I don't regret not knowing him? I was eight years old when he walked out on Mother and me, twelve before I saw him again. That hardly makes for an easy relationship.'

'But you aren't loath to take what he left you.'

Her chin lifted at that, eyes no longer their normal warm brown but sparking with tawny lights. 'I think I'm entitled, if only as some form of compensation for being robbed of a father all those years. No doubt you were hoping for the lot!'

The muscle running along his jawline tensed as his teeth came together. For a lengthy moment he allowed his gaze to rove her face, skimming over high cheekbones down to the curve of a mouth just a fraction too wide for true aesthetic appeal. The heavy rope of honey-blonde hair, at present caught back with a slide into the nape of her neck, struck a note incongruous with the classic severity of her black suit.

'I'm going to ignore that remark,' he said with control. 'Only don't take it as a sign of weakness.' He gave her no time to form any kind of reply. 'Martin wanted you to join him in the hope of trying to make things up to you. I'm not sure what prompted him to draw up his will when he did, because he couldn't have known he was going to be involved in an accident so soon afterwards, but his reasoning was sound. Given the opportunity, you'd have put your half of the business on the open market without a second thought, wouldn't you?'

'You'd have naturally been offered first refusal,' she said, unwilling to pretend otherwise.

'Always providing I could have come up with the hard cash, of course. If you knew anything at all about running a business, you'd be aware that most of the profits are ploughed right back in over the first few years in order to expand. Langhill is just . . .' He broke off, shaking his head. 'Beside the point. Your interests lie in other directions. OK, so once you reach twenty-five I shan't be able to stop you from doing as you like with your interest, but by then I'll be in a position to make you an offer you can't resist.' The last with irony. 'What you do between now and then is your own affair. If you're in need of money for day-to-day living expenses et cetera, that's obviously different.'

'I've coped on my own for the last six months,' Gina returned stiffly. 'I dare say I can go on doing it without holding out the begging bowl. Only don't think it ends here. I'll be taking independent legal advice.'

'You'll be wasting your money. Your father was in full possession of all his faculties when the will was drawn.' He drank the last of his coffee and glanced at the leather-strapped watch spanning one lean tanned wrist. 'What are your immediate plans?'

'Considering the circumstances, I don't have much choice.' She was making no effort to be gracious in defeat. 'There's a train at three.'

'It's only just gone eleven-thirty.' There was a pause, a slight change of tone. 'Time enough to take a look at Langhill first.'

'In aid of what?' she challenged. 'As you so rightly pointed out, I don't have any interest in the time-share business.'

The grey eyes could have pierced armour plating. 'As a posthumous gesture of goodwill, if you like. It's a little too late for anything else.'

Gina cut back on the all-too-ready retort. Too late. The words had a sad ring. If there would ever have come a time when she and her father might have got closer, it was something she was never to know now. Would it really hurt her to just take a look at the place he had lived and worked for these past few years? Conditions aside, he had made her future secure. There had to be gratitude for that.

'All right,' she agreed before she could change her mind again. 'Providing I make that train. It's going to be late enough when I get home as it is.'

'Someone waiting for you?' asked Nick as he came to his feet.

'I don't really think that's any of your concern,' she responded coolly, eliciting a sudden glint.

'You're lacking a fatherly hand in more ways than the one!'

'Because I'm not into telling all and sundry my business?' Gina gave him back look for look. 'You may be in control of my financial affairs, Mr Calway, but that's as far as it goes. Whatever you might think of me, it's returned with interest, I can assure you!'

'I'll make a note of it.' He indicated the door with a curt inclination of his head. 'Shall we go?'

Outside again, he said, 'I'm parked a couple of streets down. If you want to wait here, I'll pick you up.'

'I have to pick up my case from the hotel,' she rejoined, 'so I may as well walk down with you and carry on round from there.'

'Fine.' He swung across behind her to take the outer side of the pavement, lifting an eyebrow at her swift glance. 'Goes against your liberationalist grain, does it?'

'Not at all,' she said. 'Few men appreciate the difference between equality and common courtesy.'

'Meaning you prefer it both ways. That figures.'

Gina made no answer to that. Whatever she said to this man, they were unlikely to reach any kind of understanding. She regretted having agreed to make the trip out to Loch Venachar and the Langhill estate. What good could it do her when it came right down to it? He wasn't going to relent.

On the other hand, it was better than spending several hours wandering round the town on her own, she supposed. Right now, she had little interest in general sightseeing.

The car turned out to be a late-model Rover Stirling—all soft leather upholstery and walnut veneer. Obviously the business allowed a fair margin towards personal prestige, Gina reflected cynically, fastening her seat-belt as Nick started the engine. Near enough twenty-five thousand here, if she weren't mistaken. She could have coped on twenty at a pinch.

The small but comfortable hotel where she had spent the previous two nights was off Irving Place. Nick told her to stay where she was and went in to fetch her suitcase himself, stowing it on the back seat before sliding behind the wheel again.

'Hungry?' he asked. 'It's going to take a good half-hour to get out there.'

Plus the same back in again, which hardly made the trip worthwhile in terms of time, she thought, but refrained from making the point. 'I can last,' she said. 'I had a Scottish breakfast.'

'Porridge?' He sounded surprised. 'I'd have thought toast and coffee more in your line.'

'I burned it off with a work-out half an hour after it,' she returned equably. 'The best time to get the metabolism working full tilt.'

'Right enough.' There was more than a hint of amusement in the agreement. 'You seem to know your stuff OK.'

'Thanks.' She made no attempt to hide the sarcasm. 'Did you ever try aerobics yourself?'

He shook his head. 'Judo is more in my line. Same result, plus the extra bonus. You should take it up.'

'I already did.' Gina kept her tone level. 'I hold a brown belt.'

'Good going.' This time the approval was genuine. 'Every woman should have the means of self-defence in this day and age.'

'One of the classes I planned on running.' She let the remark stand for a meaningful moment but gained no notable response, adding sourly, 'I suppose you're a black belt yourself?'

The shrug was casual. 'I've been at it a long time.'

'Competitively?'

'Not these days. We opened a gymnasium ourselves last year for members' use. I give lessons a couple of times a week. And before you say what you're thinking, there's a vast difference between that and what you were proposing.'

'I'm well aware of it,' she retorted. 'I'm no part-timer. I work eight hours a day, often longer, at the club.'

He sent a swift glance. 'I thought you said there were no health clubs at present in Barchester?'

'There aren't. I travel into Cambridge. More than an hour each way.'

He made no reply to that. They had left the town and were heading through pleasant, cultivated countryside towards the higher hills and rugged mountain slopes of the Trossachs. A beautiful day in every way except the one, Gina acknowledged. Two years was a lifetime viewed from this end. At twenty-five, she had planned on being well along the path towards expansion herself, not just starting out.

Useless asking the man at her side to change his mind. He had made his position clear enough. Not that he would have any difficulty raising the money to buy her out now if he wanted to. Langhill was a going concern. The banks would fall over themselves to extend a helping hand.

She could see Nick Calway's hands out of the corner of her eye, long-fingered and with a look of tensile strength in their grasp of the wheel. Unmarried by choice rather than lack of opportunity, for sure. His type held a fatal attraction for a certain kind of woman willing to be dominated by the male.

'How did you and my father get together in the first place?' she asked curiously. 'He was quite a piece older.'

'But still on the same wavelength.' Nick slowed for the junction ahead, accelerating away again on judging the way clear. 'Some friends introduced us,' he went on. 'We were both interested in the time-share market, so we decided to pool our resources. Martin had spent some time in the States, as you'll already know, and——'

'No, I didn't know,' Gina interrupted on an edge of bitterness. 'I doubt if my mother did either.'

'Well, he had.' Nick was obviously not about to be drawn. 'So had I. We gleaned some very useful ideas over there. The upshot was we sold almost every unit within months. Right now we're in the process of building a further block of six units, due to be completed by the end of the month. We've also extended facilities. There are both indoor and outdoor heated pools, a couple of hard courts, an assault course and jogging track, a children's playground, and a new leisure centre incorporating the gymnasium, a solarium, squash courts and a sauna. The restaurant and main functions rooms are in the house itself.'

'Must really enhance the scenery,' Gina commented drily, and received a brief glance.

'Langhill has thirty-seven acres of land, much of it wooded. I think you'll find the scenery unmarred.'

'Depends on the viewpoint. I don't see the set-up you just described fading into the background all that well.'

'Wait and see.' There was no change of tone, but a definite hardening about the strong mouth. 'We've provided employment for a good number of local people, with several more jobs to come. Considering the estate was run-down and the house almost derelict, that's not a bad exchange.'

'With the reactions of others not employed by the company taken into account?'

This time the reply was short and sharp. 'If you're trying to rile me, you're going the right way about it!'

Was that what she was trying to do? Gina wondered. It wasn't like her to be so abrasive, yet everything he said rubbed her up the wrong way. Her shares in such a concern must be worth a bomb. A measly twenty thousand pounds wasn't going to break any banks.

It wasn't the money, though, so much as the realisation of how close he and her father had been, came the wry thought. Not just business partners but friends. She was jealous of that friendship—resentful of an intimacy she had been denied. Nothing could ever wholly compensate for that loss.

An apology was beyond her at the moment. She stared fixedly through the windscreen, aware without looking of the ripple of muscle in his thigh as he trod the clutch to overtake a slower-moving vehicle, and again as he dropped back into fourth gear. No automatic gearbox for Nick Calway. He would make the decisions for himself. A force to be reckoned with all the way through!

Sited right at the foot of the Highlands proper, Callandar was a busy little town of broad streets and clean stone-built houses. The heights of Ben Ledi lofted above. Shortly afterwards, they turned left and drove with tantalising glimpses of the loch visible through the trees until the road eventually wound right down along the edge of the sun-kissed waters.

Gina lowered her window to catch the scent of pine, unstinting in her appreciation of the view. Densely wooded hills crowded the far banks. The air was fresh and clear, the distances needle sharp.

A stone-pillared gateway bearing a sign lettered in gold on green with the one word 'Langhill' hove into view around the next bend. The double iron gates weren't closed.

From the entrance, a wide tarmacadamed drive swept up through landscaped gardens to the Georgian manor house which was the hub of the wheel. There were plenty of people around, some of them wearing sports gear, all of them looking in holiday mood.

A row of terraced cottages, built in the same grey stone as the original, lay off to one side of the large car park. They were approached via a separate drive, and designed to blend with the period. The roofs of other similar layouts could be glimpsed here and there between the surrounding trees.

None of it, Gina was bound to admit, hurt the eye in the way she had anticipated.

Nick parked in a reserved space alongside the huge front doors of the house, and switched off the engine.

'I'll take you round the place first,' he said, 'and then we'll have lunch. There's plenty of time. We don't need to leave until two-thirty.'

That might be cutting it a bit fine, Gina thought, but decided against any comment to that effect. If she missed the train she missed the train; she could always stay over a further night in Stirling. This was likely to be the one and only visit she ever paid to Langhill, but her financial interest was ongoing. If nothing else, she would have some idea of how the whole thing worked.

They left the main house till last. Instead, Nick walked her up to the new block of cottages at present nearing completion. The builders had knocked off work for lunch. Nick indicated for Gina to precede him through the nearest doorway.

'These are all designed to sleep up to eight people,' he said in the small square hallway from which an open pine staircase led to the upper floor. 'Others sleep four and six, depending on price per owned week. It's a lifetime ownership.'

Gina made no comment during the tour of the cottage. Although unfurnished as yet, the rooms were spacious and beautifully decorated, with fittings on a par. The sitting-room had sliding glass doors opening on to a patio cut off from its neighbours by white stone walls, while the green and white dining-kitchen boasted every aid to easy living imaginable.

Upstairs were three double bedrooms, a bathroom and a separate shower-room, with another small cloakroom and toilet downstairs completing the layout.

'I thought you said they slept up to eight people,' she queried on reaching the hallway again.

'There'll be a pull-down double bed built into a wall of units in the sitting-room,' Nick confirmed. 'Very comfortable too. I tried one out myself. Apart from the four blocks of cottages, the house has three apartments on the first floor. Staff quarters are in what used to be the attics. Not that so many live in.'

'I suppose,' she said, 'you kept one of the apartments for your own use.'

'I have a room on the upper floor too. So did your father. You might like to take a look in there—sort out a few things. It's just as he left it.'

Something closed up inside her. 'I'd feel like an intruder,' she claimed. 'He was more or less a stranger.'

'As much your fault as his these latter years.' Nick was giving no quarter. 'Right or wrong, he had his reasons for what he did. Twenty is too young for anyone to be tied down.'

'My mother was only twenty-six when she was left to bring up a child on her own,' Gina responded tautly. 'She didn't opt out on her responsibilities.'

'So hers was the stronger character.' He was beginning to sound intolerant. 'It's immaterial now, isn't it? He's gone. All that's left of him is there in that room. If you're not interested, I'll have someone clear it out.' He turned to exit through the open doorway, adding brusquely, 'We'll take a look at the leisure centre, then go find some lunch.'

Two storeys in height, the centre lay along the far side of the car park, and could also be reached from inside the house via a glassed-in corridor. The indoor swimming-pool had its twin on the other side of floor-to-ceiling windows, with the majority of people indulging at present choosing sunshine in preference to shade. Several children were at play in a separate splash pool.

Next door lay a sizeable and well-equipped gymnasium, with the sauna and solarium beyond, together with the squash courts. On the floor above was a bar plus cafeteria, and an entertainments-room capable of holding a full capacity crowd.

Gina was impressed despite herself. There had been a lot of thought put into this project, and all of it good. The gymnasium she couldn't have bettered herself. It was open to a limited outside public on payment of a membership fee, Nick told her, as were the other club facilities. It had to be made to pay for itself.

The gym instructor was just completing a work-out on one of the presses when they got downstairs again. Gina admired the compact but beautifully toned body as he came to his feet and reached for a towel. He was no more than a couple of inches taller than herself, and perhaps three or at the most four years older, his blond hair darkened by sweat. The glance he ran over her was equally assessing. His smile approved of what he saw.

'Rob McKay,' said Nick succinctly. 'This is Martin's daughter, Rob. Virginia Sutherland.'

'Gina,' corrected the latter smoothly. 'Hello, Rob.'

'Hello.' The soft Scottish burr was pleasant on the ear. 'Sorry about your father. He was a fine man. Have you come to join us?'

'Just visiting,' she said. 'Although I wouldn't have minded trying out some of the equipment.'

His interest sharpened. 'Into body-building, are you?'

She laughed. 'Only up to a point. I work in a gym myself. Mostly on aerobics.'

'That's a class we could do with setting up here,' he said. 'I've been getting enquiries every day since we opened. Not really my style.' The last with a flash of even white teeth.

'It's worth thinking about,' agreed Nick. 'And we'd better be thinking about lunch,' he added to Gina, 'if you're going to make that train.'

'You're leaving today?' Rob sounded disappointed. 'That's a shame!'

'Needs must,' she responded lightly. 'I have a job to get back to.' She held out a hand. 'Nice to have met you, anyway.'

The return pressure was firm and warm. 'Same here.'

Outside again, and moving towards the house, she said, 'You certainly don't stint on quality, I'll give you that. You have almost exactly the kind of set-up back there that I planned on having—minus the extras, that is.'

Strides toned down to correspond with hers, hands thrust casually into trouser pockets, Nick gave her an enigmatic glance. 'So why don't you take advantage of it,' he suggested, 'and stay on?'

CHAPTER TWO

GINA stopped dead in her tracks. 'Are you crazy?'

'Not at the last count.' Nick's tone was dry. 'You heard what Rob just said. What better way of indulging your interests?'

'You really think I'd settle for an offer like that?'

'Considering it's the only one I'm likely to be making, you either take it or leave it,' came the unmoved response. 'At the very least, you'd be able to keep a weather eye on your interests. Hardly a bad move.'

'Let me get this straight,' she said. 'You're suggesting I leave Barchester and move up here lock, stock and barrel?'

'In a word, yes.' Grey eyes revealed little of what was going on in the mind behind them. 'For the next two years, at any rate. After that, of course, it would be up to you.' There was a pause, a slight change of tone. 'Is there any particular reason why you wouldn't want to leave Barchester?'

'Apart from the fact that it's my home town, you mean?' The irony was intentional. 'I might be my father's daughter, but I don't have to follow in his footsteps. Joining forces with you holds no appeal whatsoever.'

'I'm offering you a job, not a full-blown partnership,' he said. 'You'd be on salary the same as Rob for the time being. The main point is you'd be here on the spot where Martin wanted you to be.'

'But not where I want to be.'

A narrowed, assessing look in his eyes, he was silent for a long moment before replying to that statement. When he did speak it was with a certain calculation. 'So, I'll make one concession. Spend a year here learning the ropes, and I'll back you in whatever you want to do at the end of it.'

Twelve months was a whole lot better than two years, Gina reflected, but still not what she wanted to hear. 'It would be a waste of time,' she appealed. 'Yours *and* mine.'

His shrug was brief. 'Your decision. Think about it over lunch.'

She didn't need to think about it, Gina told herself, falling into step with him again as he headed for the house. Leaving Cambridgeshire meant leaving Paul, and she intended doing neither. Two years or not, she would stick it out. She had to stick it out. Nick Calway had made the only allowance he was going to make. That much was only too depressingly obvious.

Inside, the house had been beautifully restored. The whole of the ground floor, including the open staircase, was thickly carpeted in woodland green, the furnishings a clever and tasteful mixture of old and new. Gina paused to admire a marquetry escritoire in the wide hallway, running a hand over the softly glowing inlay.

'It's a Beurdeley,' supplied Nick. 'I found it in a junk shop along with a load of old tables. Amazing what people will throw away.'

'Not everyone is capable of recognising an antique when they see it,' Gina returned. 'Don't you find it a risk having something like this in here when there are children running about?'

'Having a share in the place makes people think twice before letting their kids run riot. There's a collective pride in keeping the place looking good.' He added, 'Would you prefer to eat in the restaurant, or privately?'

'The restaurant, I think,' she said, somehow reluctant to be alone with him. 'Always providing there's a table available.'

'It's rarely full at lunchtime. Those who aren't out for the day often choose to use their own facilities. We don't run an extensive menu.' He was moving as he spoke, leading the way past a mahogany reception desk towards opened double doors at the far side of the hall. 'Evenings are something else. We run dinner dances on Saturdays, and bring in outside entertainment once or twice each week, so we tend to get a full complement.'

A well-organised structure all round, Gina reflected. One couldn't help but admire such enterprise. Living here would hardly be boring with so much going on. Not that she intended changing her mind on that score. Her home was in Barchester.

A folding, panelled wall cut the restaurant in half for daytime use. Gina approved the fresh cream and lemon drapes and table linen, the sparkling silver and glassware. Of the eight tables on view, only four were occupied. Nick chose one set in a window, smiling a greeting to a couple in the vicinity who obviously recognised him.

'A lot of owners join the exchange organisation,' he said, 'so we get new people coming in all the time.' He handed her a leather-bound menu. 'The trout is locally caught.'

'I'll settle for that,' she said without bothering to look at the menu. Her gaze went to the window

with its view out over a wide terrace to lawns and
flower gardens. 'You've certainly made a wonderful
job of it all. I'm not surprised people were eager
to buy in.'

'What was done once can always be done again,'
came the level return. 'There's a place on the coast
that's ripe for a similar conversion.'

Brown eyes darkened as she looked at him. 'So
that's the real reason you're so reluctant to part
with any money!'

'The real reason,' he stated grimly, 'lies back
there in the will your father left. We planned all
along on expanding to other venues.'

'You could give me use of twenty-five thousand
without even feeling it,' she came back, and saw
the firm mouth stretch in a humourless smile.

'Until you needed more—which you more than
likely would. Budgets have a way of expanding too.
My previous offer still stands. One year. You could
learn a lot that might stand you in good stead.' He
looked up to smile at the young waitress halting at
his side with pad and pencil poised. 'We'll both have
the melon and the trout, thank you, Sue.'

The temptation to say yes and have done with it
almost got the better of her. Gina stared fixedly at
her plate, trying to get to grips with the overall
problem. Paul had been the one to point out her
right to this inheritance, yes, but how would he feel
if she upped sticks and left him for a year? She
certainly wouldn't like it herself were the positions
reversed.

'I'd need to think about it,' she said when the
waitress had departed.

Nick studied her thoughtfully, giving little away.
'How long?'

She shrugged. 'A few days, at least. It isn't an easy decision to make.'

'So think about it,' he said. 'You know where to contact me.'

He left the subject alone after that. Lunch over, he made no further attempt to persuade her to take a look at her father's things, but suggested they make for Stirling and her train. Gina wasn't loath to agree. She needed to be alone with her fluctuating thoughts.

The journey home would at least provide her with the opportunity to view the prospect from all sides and work out just what she was going to say to Paul when she saw him. His opinion had to be taken into consideration. Sharing decisions was a vital part of any stable relationship.

They made the train with five minutes to spare. Nick said goodbye at the barrier with a brief handshake and an injunction to take care. His departure left her feeling somehow depleted.

Sinking into a seat, she tried to bring her mind to bear on the factors involved in his offer. Living up here amid this kind of scenery would be no hardship, true. Neither was use of the estate facilities to be sneezed at. And working alongside someone like Rob McKay would be a pleasure in itself.

Which still left Paul to be considered. Could their relationship survive the distance?

The journey involved two changes and not a little time-wasting. By the time she had reached Barchester, it was gone nine o'clock. Paul would, she knew, be waiting for her phone call. Feeling more like a comforting cocoa and bed, Gina dialled the number. It would be unfair to make him wait until morning to hear how she had got on.

His voice on the line sounded just a little aggrieved. 'I thought you might have phoned before this,' he said, 'just to put me in the picture. How did it go?'

'As well as funerals can go, I suppose,' Gina returned. 'It wasn't a lavish affair. Apart from Nick Calway, there was only a handful of people there.'

'It wasn't the funeral I was asking about,' he responded. 'People who cut themselves off from family the way your father did can hardly expect a tearful and loving send-off. You've seen the solicitor dealing with the probate?'

'Yes.' Gina hesitated before continuing, aware of his likely reaction. 'It isn't quite as straightforward as it first appeared. Father made Nick Calway trustee until I'm twenty-five.'

'The hell he did!' Relatively mild though it was, the profanity sounded strange on Paul's lips. 'That was a lousy trick!'

Without thinking about it, Gina found herself leaping to her father's defence. 'Not really. After all, he had little idea of what I might be likely to do, given a free rein.'

'That's hardly the point. Imposing conditions from the grave is hardly playing fair.' There was a pause, an obvious and rapid assessment of ideas. 'We'll have to fight it.'

'We?' Gina's tone was soft, but the inflexion came through, eliciting a hasty retraction.

'I meant you, of course. All the same, you're going to need help.'

'I'm not sure,' she said slowly, 'that I want to fight it, Paul. If that was the way my father wanted it——'

The interruption came terse. 'You mean the way he was probably pressured into it! This partner of his—what kind of man is he?'

'Not the kind you're hinting at.' She could say that with conviction. 'He doesn't get anything out of it.'

'Apart from another two years in total control.' He added decisively, 'We can't talk this through on the phone. I'm coming over.'

'Tonight? It's already gone half-past nine!'

The pause was timed. 'I can always stay.'

Gina sighed. 'We've had this out before. You know my views.'

'Extremely old-fashioned ones.'

'So you've told me. The fact remains that I prefer to wait until we're married before we start sharing a bed. It might be a lot to ask, but that's the way it is.'

'If I didn't know different, I'd say you were under-sexed,' he complained. 'How any girl can kiss a man the way you kiss me and not want to take things further is beyond me!'

Looking for something she had yet to find, came the fleeting thought, hastily pushed to the back of her mind where it could do least harm. 'It's called control,' she said shortly, and then on a note of apology, 'I can't help the way I'm made. As a matter of fact, Nick came up with a proposal worth thinking about. He said if I were prepared to spend the next year up there at Langhill, he'd be prepared to make concessions with regard to my plans.'

'What good would that do?' Paul's tone was blank. 'You're not intending going into the time-share business.'

'It's rather more than just a holiday set-up.' Gina reconciled herself to a lengthy discourse. Best now while it was still fresh in her mind than waiting until tomorrow. 'Apart from learning about the overall business, I'd be gaining some valuable experience in my own line.'

She went on to describe what Langhill was about, gaining enthusiasm by the minute as she did so. 'The facilities are second to none,' she finished, 'with a ready-made clientele on a year-round basis. I realise we wouldn't be seeing a great deal of each other during the twelve months, but the routes are good. You could always come up for the occasional weekend—or even longer if you got the chance.'

It was a few seconds before he made any reply. When he did speak it was on an odd note. 'You seem to have already decided to accept the offer.'

Up until that moment, Gina hadn't been aware of having done so. It was almost a relief to have the matter resolved for her.

'It's too good a chance to turn down,' she acknowledged. 'Twelve months isn't all that long to wait—especially as I shan't be time-wasting during it.' She hesitated before tagging on, 'What do you think?'

'Does it make any difference?' The odd note was still there. 'If you've already made up your mind, there's nothing much I can do but accept it. Maybe it mightn't be such a bad move, at that. I'd be interested to see the place for myself. When were you thinking of going?'

Gina hadn't thought about it at all as yet. The speed with which Paul appeared to not only have come round to the idea but be positively eager to see her on her way made her blink.

'I'd have to discuss it with Nick Calway,' she acknowledged slowly. 'I told him I needed time to think about it.'

'So tell him in the morning. There's nothing to keep you from leaving fairly soon. A week's notice should suffice for the club, and your landlord will be more than ready to re-let the flat at an increased rent.' The enthusiasm was his now. 'I'll help you straighten things up down here.'

'Thanks.' The irony in her voice was too faint to be transmitted over the line. 'I'll need all the help I can get.'

'See you tomorrow, then.' Paul sounded animated. 'We have a lot to talk about.'

Gina failed to see what. It all seemed to have been said. Tomorrow she would telephone Nick and tell him her decision. She could only hope she was making the right one.

Arriving at Stirling station for the second time in less than a fortnight, Gina had an odd sense of coming home. Odd, because home was several hundred miles away, and a whole year distant. Viewed from this end, that year seemed to stretch to infinity. What she had to do was fix her mind on the eventual gain to be made in the shape of her own business. Once there, she wouldn't be looking back.

True to his word, Paul had made every effort to help her over the minor hurdles presented by a hurried departure north. He was going to miss her, he had said last night, but future security had to come first and foremost. In any case, he would be seeing her at the end of the month for a long weekend.

Studying the good-looking features beneath the smooth sweep of fair hair, Gina had wondered at her own lack of despondency in leaving him. That she was envied her association with Paul by several of her friends she was too well aware. That at least two would be more than ready to step into her shoes given any opportunity at all she was also aware. The possibility that Paul himself might well respond to any such overtures in her absence she resolutely struck from her mind. Trust went both ways—or it should.

Emerging through the barrier, she was both surprised and a little disturbed to see Nick Calway himself standing there waiting. Today he was dressed casually and comfortably in trousers and lightweight jacket, but looked no less a man of substance. He came forward to take the single suitcase from her hand, hefting it for weight with a quizzical expression in his eyes. 'Is this all?'

'All I've brought with me,' Gina acknowledged. 'The rest is coming on by carrier.'

'Sounds ominous.' He was turning as he spoke to move in the direction of the station exit. 'I'm parked down the road a way. If you want to wait, I'll fetch the car round.' His mouth slanted. 'I seem to remember going down that road before. No doubt you'd as soon walk with me.'

'Always providing I can manage the distance.' Gina wasn't about to rise to the taunt. 'It's good of you to take the time to meet me. I could have come in by taxi.'

'No trouble. If we're going to be partners, we have to help each other.'

She gave him a swift sideways glance. 'Is that what we are?'

The shrug was casual. 'On paper, at least. You own an equal interest.' He changed the suitcase over to the other hand. 'Not quite as light as I thought. Bring your dumb-bells with you?'

'Few people call them anything but hand weights these days,' she returned on a scathing note, and saw the sardonic smile come again.

'Call it a slip of the tongue. Rob was delighted to know you'd be joining him. The two of you should be able to provide a full programme between you.'

'I'm looking forward to it.' That much Gina could say with truth. For the rest, she still entertained serious doubts. Nick wasn't going to be the easiest person with whom to live and work. He was far too much of the cynic for her taste.

Today, the weather lacked the pure perfection of last time, although the sun kept peering out from behind the cloud cover. Robbed of the latter, the landscape looked rather more sombre. But then so did anywhere under cloudy skies, Gina reminded herself, trying to retain some measure of good spirits. One short year. She could withstand anything Nick cared to throw at her in the knowledge that an end was in sight.

They reached Langhill at four o'clock to see a laughing crowd of people just emerging from the leisure centre.

'We had a swimming gala scheduled for this afternoon,' Nick volunteered. 'Always a popular event—especially the children's races.' He parked the car in his reserved space, and switched off the engine. 'I'll take you up to your room first, then we'll have some tea.'

There were more people on view inside the house today too. Some were just using the facilities for sitting, some for conversing; others seemed to have no fixed plan in mind. The bar was off to the left of the main lounge. Gina could hear the hum of voices, a sudden burst of laughter. A good time was obviously being had by all.

'We've a pretty gregarious crowd in this week,' commented Nick as they mounted the sweep of a staircase together. 'Some people are rarely seen outside their private accommodation. Not that there's anything wrong in that, of course. Each to their own. That's what it's all about.'

'You certainly seem to cater for all tastes,' Gina agreed.

'We,' he corrected. 'Martin and I were in full accord—including, as I've said before, future plans.'

'You obviously both had your sights set on becoming millionaires,' she said drily, and saw his lip tilt.

'You could say that too. Nothing wrong in a little healthy ambition. You're a case in point yourself.'

Her laugh sounded brittle. 'Not to quite the same extent. I'd be happy with just the one outlet.'

'Initially, maybe. You're not the type to settle for half a loaf.'

'You don't know me,' Gina retorted.

'I knew your father pretty well, and you come across as very much like him in temperament.' Nick's tone took on a dryness of its own. 'Apart from the touchiness, that is. I'm not criticising. Without ambition, we'd still be living in caves.'

Some, she thought with asperity, might be better suited to that venue! She refrained from further comment. Sarcasm would get her precisely nowhere with this man. She didn't have to like him, but she did have to learn to live with him—loosely speaking, that was.

They mounted to the second floor via a narrower staircase obviously once meant for the servants. There was a lift, Nick advised, but it was normally only used for the carrying of luggage and other heavy items.

The room to which he showed her was light and airy and surprisingly spacious. A dormer window framed a wonderful view out over the whole loch. Looking at it, Gina felt her spirits lift. Who could possibly stay indifferent to scenery such as this?

'We managed to incorporate a shower-room and toilet facilities in each of the staff quarters,' said Nick from the doorway. 'A bit cramped, maybe, but adequate. I'm right next door, if you ever have need of company.'

Gina turned to look back at him, noting the faint twist to his lips. 'I'm quite self-sufficient, thanks,' she returned coolly. 'Do I take it this was my father's room?'

His shrug was answer enough. 'I had it cleared out for you. There should be no reminders left to haunt your dreams.' He straightened away from the jamb where he had been leaning a shoulder. 'Come on down to the office when you're ready, and we'll have that tea.' He began to turn, adding without change of inflexion, 'Amber looks good with your colouring. Less ageing than the black.'

He was gone before she could find a reply—if there was a reply to that comment. Involuntarily she found herself glancing at the long mirror on one side-wall, assessing the reflected image with a sudden new critique.

There was nothing wrong with her figure, she already knew; she had made certain of that since first acquiring an interest in keep-fit in her teens. Facially, she was far from satisfied, but, short of plastic surgery, one had to make the most of what was given in that sphere. Her mouth was too wide, her eyes too cat-like in their slightly slanted set, her cheekbones a fraction too prominent.

Her hair was definitely her best feature. Thick and glossy, it hung straight as a die to her shoulder-blades. There had been a time when she could sit on it, but even her mother had been forced to agree that she couldn't go through life carrying that same Garden-of-Eden style. Even now it had to be washed every other day to keep it looking good. Time-consuming, but worthwhile.

As this whole move had to be worthwhile if it got her where she wanted to be, she reflected, dismissing her appearance in favour of more pressing matters. A year of her life was nothing compared with what she stood to gain.

CHAPTER THREE

DECORATED and furnished to a standard more than adequate to her needs, the room, Gina found, was quite satisfactory. Even the knowledge that her father had occupied the place before her was somehow no longer off-putting.

The sofa set against one wall pulled out into a double bed. Apart from this there was an armchair, a chest of drawers which also doubled as a dressing-table via the mirror hung above it, a built-in wardrobe along another wall, and a couple of occasional tables. The carpet was fitted and a warm golden brown in colour to tone with the pale gold curtains at the window.

Reached via a sliding door, the shower room proved more functional than fancy, but it sufficed. Gina resisted the temptation to take a shower here and now and change her clothing, contenting herself instead with a quick hand wash and a freshening up of her lipstick.

She found herself looking forward with some degree of pleasure to meeting up with Rob again, and trying out the club facilities at first hand. That probably wouldn't be before morning, of course. Tonight she would have enough to contend with in the shape of Nick Calway himself. The tea he had mentioned hardly fitted her emerging idea of the man. Probably a gesture for her benefit. Not that he needed to bother trying to make her feel at home. Her position was purely temporary.

She found the office off the rear of the main hallway. Seated at a right-angled desk, the strikingly attractive brunette at present working on a word-processor looked round at Gina's entry, her expression undergoing a distinct and far from welcoming alteration.

'You must be Martin's daughter,' she said coolly. 'Nick is through in the sitting-room. I'll order tea now you're here.'

Finally. Unspoken, the word hung in the air like an accusation of tardiness. Gina forced herself to ignore the chilly reception. That the woman actively resented her presence was only too obvious, although the reason was less clear. Around twenty-six or -seven in years, the other gave an impression of ownership. Her use of first names where both Nick and Gina's father were concerned certainly implied a somewhat closer relationship than a mere employee might enjoy.

'Thanks,' Gina replied without particular inflexion. 'Which door?'

A brief inclination of the smooth dark head indicated the second of the two on offer. 'Through there.'

Gina moved towards it without a further glance in the other's direction. Two could play that game. Opening the door, she found herself in a small but pleasantly furnished room overlooking the rear of the house. Nick got to his feet from the chair where he was leafing through a sheaf of papers, grey eyes registering a certain calculation as he appraised her.

'Everything OK?'

'Fine.' Gina was determined to show nothing but appreciation: not a difficult task, considering. She closed the door in her wake, added lightly, 'Who's the daughter of joy outside?'

The satire aroused no more than a faint flick of an eyebrow. 'Fiona Gordon. She's my secretary-cum-PA. There's only a few years between you. You might find her a useful friend.'

Not, thought Gina with emphasis, in a *million* years! If ever she had experienced an instant incompatibility, it was out there in that office. Hardly important anyway. If she needed a friend in camp, Rob McKay would be a far better choice.

'This is nice,' she said, looking around the room. 'You do yourself proud.'

'Martin and I shared the place,' came the level response. 'Feel free to use it yourself whenever.'

'Thanks.' Gina already regretted the ungracious comment, although she wasn't relaxed enough to unbend completely. She added quickly, 'I'm looking forward to getting to work. I have a programme worked out. Perhaps Rob and I could go over it tomorrow.'

'Saturday is change-over day, and the centre is closed for cleaning,' he said. 'Better make it Sunday morning. It will give me time to go through the general set-up with you. There's a whole lot more to running this kind of concern than meets the eye.'

'I can believe it.' Gina had already determined to make no demur over anything she was called upon to imbibe during her time here at Langhill. At the very least, it would be interesting.

She crossed to the window to gaze over the spacious rose garden enclosed within hedges of yew. 'Just keeping the grounds up to scratch must be a full-time job.'

'It is. We employ an outside firm to take care of it.'

Nick had come up behind her, standing close enough for her to feel the warmth from his body—to catch the faint and purely masculine scent of his aftershave. A man to beware of, came the unbidden and unwanted thought. A man almost too male for comfort. A sudden *frisson* ran the length of her spine. She felt hemmed in by forces new to her.

'You have the most beautiful hair,' he said softly and unexpectedly, and ran a hand over it as if to emphasise the point. 'Is the colour natural?'

'Yes.' The word came out clipped, though not with indignation. 'I'm not into false impressions.'

'Not exactly the truth.' His voice had crispened again. 'You didn't let on that you were seriously involved with anyone.'

She stiffened. 'How——?'

'He phoned me last week. Asked some pretty searching questions.' The pause was brief. 'You didn't ask him to?'

'Not in so many words.' Gina kept her anger well under control. What did Paul think he was playing at? 'He's naturally concerned for my welfare,' she tagged on, for want of anything more plausible to say. 'He was probably just trying to make sure everything was above board.'

'You still have doubts yourself?'

'No.' Too close or not, she made herself turn. 'I was out of order the other week. Da...my father had every right to do as he thought fit.'

'Let yourself go for once and call him Dad,' Nick advised on a dry note. 'It's easier on the tongue.' He hadn't moved an inch; so near that she could see tiny green specks in the grey of his eyes. 'I'm glad to see you're coming round to realising he wasn't such a bad type after all.'

'Nothing can excuse the fact that he deprived me of a father and Mom of a husband all those years, but there's no point in continuing to be bitter about it.'

Gina wanted desperately to step past him, only there was no way of doing it without underlining her reluctance to be this near to him. His mouth was on a level with her eyes, the lips so firmly moulded and decisive. For a fleeting moment she wondered what it would be like to have them on hers.

The opening of the door and entry of Fiona carrying a tray brought a mixture of relief and regret—the latter because she had an odd feeling that she had been about to have curiosity satisfied. Nick swung round in apparent surprise to see his PA performing menial tasks.

'Someone else could have done that,' he said.

'They're all busy,' came the answer. Not a hair out of place, the woman laid the tray down on the coffee-table and straightened, her glance flickering from one to the other of them in narrowed speculation. 'I have those letters ready for signing, Nick,' she added, once again giving Gina the impression that she used the name with purpose.

'Fine; I'll come and see to it now, then you can get them in tonight's post.' He was moving as he spoke. 'Help yourself, Gina. I'll only be a couple of minutes.'

Fiona made a point of closing the door as she left the room in Nick's wake. Left alone, Gina took advantage of the invitation to go across and pour herself a cup of tea. There was a small plate of sandwiches too, along with another of fancy cakes. Glancing at her watch, she was surprised to see it was only just gone five o'clock. A lot seemed to have happened since her arrival.

Thinking about the last few minutes brought a tensing of stomach muscle. That she was physically attracted to Nick she could no longer deny, though it wasn't what she wanted to feel. Had he known exactly what was going through her mind back there? A man like Nick Calway would always know when a woman was responding to him. He had probably found it amusing.

It was more like ten minutes before he returned. Taking a seat in the chair opposite her own, he reached for a sandwich but declined her offer to pour him some tea.

'Not my tipple,' he said, confirming her prior assessment. 'I'm more a coffee man myself.'

'Too much caffeine is bad for you,' Gina advised automatically, and felt herself colour as he directed an ironic glance.

'It would be a dull life if we only did what was good for us.'

'But a safe one.'

He shrugged and smiled. 'Each to their own. I don't smoke, or drink alcohol to excess.'

'You left out women,' she retorted, and saw the smile take on a new twist.

'I left out song too, but I was never much for the school choir.' His gaze went over her as she sat there with the early evening light from the window behind her outlining her features. 'What about this Paul Milton character? Are you planning on marrying him?'

Gina refrained with an effort from suggesting that he mind his own business. 'We haven't made any definite plans as yet,' she said. 'I'd hoped to have the club up and running before that.'

'He didn't object to losing you for a year?'

'Not under the circumstances. Anyway, he hasn't lost me, as you put it. He'll be coming up from time to time.' She added levelly, 'I take it you've no objection to that?'

Some unreadable expression crossed the lean features. 'Would I try to mar the progress of true love?'

'I think,' she said with acerbity, 'you'd do anything you wanted, whoever else suffered.'

His mouth took on an ironic line. 'As you so rightly said earlier, we barely know one another. Let's agree to withhold judgement until proven, shall we?' He gave her no time to respond. 'To answer the question seriously, I've no objection to his visiting the place, always providing we have a bed going spare. Unless you're prepared to share yours, of course.'

'No, I'm not!' The denial was more forceful than she had intended, drawing a raised brow and another shrug of broad shoulders.

'Just a thought. Nothing to get worked up about. We'll sort something out when the time comes. Is it likely to be soon?'

'The end of the month.' Gina hesitated before tagging on, 'What exactly *did* Paul ask you?'

'I've already told you. He wanted to know the pros and cons of time-share. Judging from the questions he came up with, he'd been doing some prior homework.'

'You gave him the answers?'

'I don't discuss my affairs over the phone with someone I've never even met.'

His tone had hardened. Enough so to give Gina pause before she spoke again. 'If Paul and I are going to be married, he has a right to be interested in *my* affairs.'

' "If" being the operative word. You don't strike me as being in any way ready for marriage.'

'And you'd know so much about it!' She was sitting bolt upright in the chair, twin flags of colour highlighting her cheekbones. 'I'm more than capable of deciding that for myself, thanks!'

'I doubt it.' He was totally unmoved by the display of temper. 'I'd say you should wait until you're at least a couple of years older before tying that particular knot.'

'Until you're no longer in a position to have any say—is that what you're getting at?'

'If you like. Not that Martin's will gave me any jurisdiction over your love-life. All I can offer is advice.'

'Which I can get along just fine without, thank you.' Gina made no effort to soften the rebuttal. 'I'm not some silly kid with stars in her eyes! Marriage is a partnership, not a take-over.'

'Total equality doesn't work,' he came back imperturbably. 'You only have to look at today's divorce rate to have that fact confirmed. Women always think they know exactly what they want in a man until they get it, by which time it's usually too late. A clever woman will always allow her man to appear top dog even if she's the real backbone of the family.'

'Poppycock!' Gina was too incensed by what she considered the pure patronisation to take a humorous view. 'I'd stay single all my life rather than kowtow to a man simply because he happens to be male!'

'Maybe because you never came across one capable of evoking a healthy respect.'

There was no doubting the amusement in his tone now. Gina bit her lip, aware of being deliberately baited. She wasn't usually so slow on the uptake, but then she had never met anyone so totally infuriating as Nick Calway before.

'God help any woman *you* marry,' was all she could find to say. She got to her feet. 'I'll go and unpack.'

Nick stayed where he was, the disturbing glint still there in his eyes. 'Good idea. Dinner is from seven until ten. You will be eating here, I imagine?'

Already on her way to the door, she said shortly, 'Where else?'

'The same table we occupied the last time, then,' he said. 'It's reserved for management.'

Gina made no answer to that. As he had set no time, she could only assume he had no intention of joining her. A relief, she told herself emphatically. She might even get to enjoy the meal.

Fiona was no longer at her desk, and the cover was on her VDU. No doubt she had left for the day. With any luck, Gina reflected, she would be gone for the whole weekend. The other's attitude was hardly scheduled to improve the situation. Her propitious arrival with the tea had smacked more of a desire to discover what was going on than a shortage of service. There had been more than a hint of proprietorship in the way she had both spoken of and to Nick. If there was anything going on between the two of them, good luck to them! They deserved one another.

It took relatively little time to unpack the one suitcase she had brought with her. There were two more to come. They should be here tomorrow. The flat had been rented furnished, so at least she didn't have storage costs to think about. Whether the premises on which she had based her original plans would still be up for grabs in a year's time was open to serious doubt, but there would be other opportunities. She could get Paul to start looking once she was within reasonable sight of the end.

With her things unpacked and put away, it was still only just gone six. Staying up here in her room until seven or later seemed a waste of time and opportunity when there were so many other ways of employing both. A swim wouldn't go amiss. Indoors today, considering the cooler temperature.

She chose a one-piece suit in turquoise, and donned a matching track-suit over it. There were sure to be changing cabins available where she could leave the latter. Taking a towel from the shower-room, she made her way downstairs again.

The hall and main rooms were well-populated, with the bar doing good business, judging from the sounds issuing forth. May was obviously a popular month for the area. As Nick had said that almost all weeks had been sold, Gina could only assume that the winter season was equally popular, if for different reasons. The leisure centre would certainly still be an attraction.

There were few people to be seen outside. Many would have retired to their own quarters to prepare the evening meal, she supposed. Handy having the choice, especially where it came to families with children in tow.

Both indoor and outdoor pools were unoccupied at present. Gina left her track-suit and towel in one of the women's changing cabins off to the rear of the premises, and fastened her hair in a thick swirl on top of her head before taking a running dive into the water at the seven-foot level. She swam several lengths in a fast crawl before pausing for a breather.

Standing on the side some short distance away, Rob McKay brought both hands together in smiling approval. 'Nice style!'

'Lots of practice,' Gina responded. 'I thought everyone had gone for the day.'

'I usually seize the chance of a quiet session while they're all busy getting ready for the evening. It gets a bit crowded in here at times. Glad you decided to join us after all,' he added. 'I've already posted the news regarding the aerobics classes. You're going to have a full list from day one, if the response is anything to go by.'

'That's great!' She hauled herself out on to the side as he moved towards her, admiring the clean lines of his body. While lacking Nick's height, he was still in perfect proportion.

Why, she wondered vexedly at that point, was she relating everything back to Nick Calway? He was no model of perfection, in any sphere!

'Nick said you planned on being with us at least a year,' Rob said now, dropping to a seat beside her. 'Your father would have been delighted to see you taking an interest.'

'Don't you start on that tack too,' she returned wryly. 'I'm already feeling guilty enough for not making the effort earlier while there was still time.'

'There's nobody ever lost anyone yet without feeling regret over the things they might have done and didn't,' came the comforting response. 'You're here now, that's all that matters.'

'How well did you know my father?' Gina asked impulsively.

'Well enough to be good and thrown when he died. He and Nick have made Langhill the best-run concern of its kind, and that's not just an opinion. The two of them worked well together.'

She kicked idly at the water, watching the droplets fly. 'Do you get along with Nick OK too?'

'Fine. He leaves me to run my own show without interference.'

'But he does give judo lessons, I believe?'

'Twice a week. He's a black belt, third dan. I'd like to see him up against some real competition, but the highest level we've ever had up here was only a blue belt.'

'You're not into the martial arts yourself, then?'

He shook his head. 'No time. I've a full programme.' Sliding down into the water, he held out an inviting hand. 'How about a little competition of our own?'

'Against those shoulders?' It was Gina's turn to shake her head, laughing as she did so. 'Unfair advantage!'

Rob grinned back. 'I'll give you a three-yard start.'

'Make it three lengths, and I might take you up on it,' she said. 'I don't like losing.'

'Especially to the male of the species.' The new voice came from behind her, too mockingly familiar for any mistake to be made. 'Faint heart never won anything.'

Gina had stiffened involuntarily on the first syllable. She made herself relax and turn her head smoothly to look at the man who stepped into view at her side, wondering why Rob hadn't given any indication of his presence.

From this angle, Nick seemed to tower over her, the plain black trunks emphasising the narrowness of hip and taut muscularity of stomach, along with other masculine attributes that brought a sudden and totally unwonted warmth to her cheeks. His shoulders were broader even than Rob's, the muscle development not quite as heavy but no less powerful in degree.

'Seems I chose the wrong time,' she said, choosing attack as a means of covering her momentary confusion. 'I'll leave you *males* to your chest-beating and try again later.'

'Hey!' Rob sounded more than a little confused himself. 'What did *I* do?'

'Nothing that can't be put right,' said Nick. There was a glint in the grey eyes. 'The pool is big enough to take all three of us without getting in one another's way.'

He moved a couple of feet away to take a standing dive, cleaving the surface with scarcely a splash to continue swimming under water down the full length of the pool.

'You two don't seem too friendly,' commented Rob lightly. 'Clashing of personalities?'

'You could call it that.' Gina smiled and shrugged. 'Nothing to worry about.'

'As half-owner, I don't imagine you've much to worry about at all,' he said. 'It's a going concern.'

Eyes on the man surfacing at the far end of the pool, she said levelly, 'I'm only just beginning to realise to what extent.' She paused, wanting to ask the question yet reluctant to show too much interest. Voice as casual as she could make it, she added, 'This secretary, Fiona—has she been here long?'

'Six months, give or take a week. The previous one left to get married.' There was something evasive in the way he left the subject. 'Are you coming in, or would you rather I took off?'

Gina shelved any further questions for another time, if at all. Whatever the relationship between Fiona Gordon and Nick, it wasn't her concern. She wouldn't allow it to be of concern.

Sliding into the water, she struck out in a leisurely breast-stroke. Rob kept pace with her for a moment or two before allowing his natural vigour to get the better of him, turning on to his back to pull away in a powerful butterfly. Gina felt her hair beginning to escape from its clip, and trod water to secure it again. The feel of a hand across her rear end stiffened her whole body in shock. Her head went under and she tasted chlorine in her mouth before jerking herself back into motion.

Surfacing right in front of her, Nick gave her a narrow smile. 'Tempt me again and you'll get the same on dry land!'

Still spluttering from the mouthful of water she had taken in, she could hardly get the words out. 'Who the hell do you think you are?'

'Simple,' he said. 'I'm the man who holds your future in the palm of his hand for the next two years. Try remembering it occasionally.'

Rob had reached the far end of the pool and was on his way back. Smarting more from the implication than the cushioned slap, Gina turned away from her partner and made for the side, hauling herself out without a backward glance.

Difficult to stalk off with dignity in a swim-suit and bare feet, she realised immediately, but it was too late to do anything but keep going. She knew Nick was watching her, and could sense his sardonic expression. That didn't help her equilibrium any either. Damn the man! He went too far. Let him keep his dominant male act for those who might appreciate it!

She was still seething, though outwardly calm, when she emerged from the changing-rooms dressed once more in the turquoise track-suit. The two men were engaged in conversation, and didn't notice her leaving. Going out, she met a middle-aged couple coming in, answering their cheerful greeting with a smile and a pleasant word of her own. Owners or exchangers, they merited civility. She represented the management now.

There was no sign of Nick when she went down at eight for dinner. Forty-five minutes later, when she left, he still hadn't put in appearance, from which it could be construed that he either wasn't eating at Langhill at all or was deliberately waiting until he thought she might be through. The former seemed the more likely. If there were any discomfiture to be felt, it would be hers not his.

It would take a great deal to put Nick Calway off his stroke, but she would find a way, Gina vowed, if it was the last thing she did!

CHAPTER FOUR

SATURDAY was warm and sunny and spirit-lifting. Impossible, Gina thought, going down to breakfast, to feel anything but anticipatory on a morning like this. True, she wouldn't be able to get to grips with her main interest until tomorrow, but once into a routine she could let everything else take a back seat—Nick included.

All the same, she was a little disconcerted to see him already seated at table, along with an auburn-haired young woman wearing a smart grey suit.

'This is Deirdre Andrews from reception,' he said as Gina pulled out a chair prior to sitting down. 'She's going to take you through the check-out detail this morning, ready for the new lot checking in after four o'clock.'

Around Gina's own age, Deirdre proffered a warm and genuine smile. 'Hello. Sorry to butt in on your breakfast, but Nick asked me to be here early.'

Apparently everyone here was on first-name terms with the boss, Gina reflected, summoning a suitable reply. Not that she found that distasteful, but simply puzzling in a man who, by his own admittance, put a healthy respect high on his list of priorities. She met the grey eyes without a flicker. Amazing what a good night's sleep could do for composure. She felt fit for anything this morning. Certainly capable of handling a receptionist's workload.

'You realise, of course, that I'm not going to have all that much free time once I get started across at the gym?' she said. 'I'm planning on just the one session a day to begin with, until I see how it's going to build up, but there'll be other exercise programmes as well.'

'Rob already does that,' Nick rejoined.

'He can continue to do it for the men; I'll take over the women.' Gina kept her tone as level as his. 'We'll be working as a team. When do you hold your judo sessions, by the way?'

'Monday and Thursday mornings,' came the reply. 'Both sexes.'

'I wasn't thinking of muscling in,' she denied. 'I'm hardly in your league.'

'A brown belt should be capable of putting up a fair degree of competition.' The casual note was belied by the taunt in his eyes. 'You'll have to show me what you can do. How about tomorrow morning before breakfast? The centre isn't open to the public until eight. Say seven-ish?'

Not for anything, Gina decided, was she going to show reluctance. 'If you like,' she agreed. 'Although my judogi is in the luggage still to come.'

'It should arrive today. If it doesn't, we keep a stock for hire.' He ran an appraising glance over that portion of her body visible above the table. 'Size twelve, I'd say. No problem.'

'I'm taking lessons myself,' put in Deirdre. 'Self-defence more than anything.' She added with enthusiasm, 'I'll be joining in the aerobics too, when I can manage it.'

'It might be an idea to hold an early evening session for those unable to make it during the day,'

Nick suggested. 'Not just staff, although they'd no doubt appreciate it.'

One thing he wasn't going to do was take over her time-table, Gina thought wrathfully, even if the idea was a good one.

'I'll consider it,' she said. 'It would have to depend on how many were interested.'

Deirdre looked from one to the other as if she sensed the hostility, if not quite understanding it, then tactfully changed the subject. Catching Nick's faint smile, Gina resisted the temptation to kick the ankle she could feel stretched out, man-like, to encroach on her space beneath the table. That would not only be childish, but might very well earn her an instant and like retaliation. Nick Calway was no gentleman when it came to dealing with the opposite sex.

She saw little of him during the rest of the morning. Reception not only dealt with people checking in and out, but a thousand and one other details too. By lunchtime, with all those due to leave despatched on their way, and the paperwork in order, Gina was more than ready for a break.

The general staff used a separate dining-room at the rear of the house. She elected to join them rather than risk spending an hour exchanging pleasantries with Nick across a table for two.

Tonight was the dinner dance, she recalled. Whether the same table would still be reserved or turned over to the general clientele was immaterial because she didn't intend dining in the restaurant. If the cafeteria across at the centre was closed, she would simply call for a taxi to take her into Callander. Whatever the cost, it would be worth it just to escape the man she was coming to detest with renewed intensity.

There was a steady flow of people checking in from four o'clock onwards, some of them owners, others taking advantage of the exchange facility which enabled them to trade off their own time-share week or weeks against a world-wide choice.

One American couple, fitting in a first-time-ever visit to Scotland as part of a European tour, professed themselves in absolute raptures over having managed to secure a week at Langhill. They knew people who had been trying for an exchange since the place opened, they said, but apparently so relatively few Langhill owners cared to go elsewhere.

'I'll be taking full advantage of the health club,' declared the middle-aged, beautifully dressed and coiffured woman as Gina handed over the key to their cottage, along with a help file of fact-sheets and maps of the area. She laughed. 'I have to get rid of the pounds I put on with all that pasta in Italy before I go back home!'

Gina smiled back. 'We'll soon do that, Mrs Graham. Can I book you in for the dinner dance tonight? There are a couple of tables still vacant.'

'Sounds good,' she agreed, giving her husband no opportunity to veto the suggestion. 'We'll be there.'

Deirdre gave Gina a thumbs-up sign as the couple moved away. 'One more to go and we have a full house!'

Gina said casually, 'I gather the staff table comes under general usage on Saturdays.'

'Unless it's specifically requested. Nick occasionally takes it.'

'On his own?'

Deirdre laughed and shook her head. 'He doesn't go short of company.'

'I can imagine.' Gina wanted to ask if said company was always the same person, having already assumed that it would certainly be female, but the question was too open to misconstruction. The last thing she needed was to have anyone believe her interested in Nick from a personal angle.

The receptionist scheduled for late duty came on at five-thirty. Free for the rest of the weekend, Deirdre was to spend Sunday rambling with friends.

'You should come with us some time,' she invited Gina as the two of them took their leave. 'They're a good crowd. You wouldn't feel out of it.'

'That would be nice,' Gina said, and meant it. 'Only I'd better find my feet down here first, I think.'

With both pools closed for cleaning, a swim was obviously out. She settled for a shower instead, and spent the next hour lying on her bed reading through the resort literature.

There was certainly no shortage of things to do and see in the area, she conceded. Glasgow, with its famed exhibition centre, was only thirty miles away, although one would never guess that close a proximity to a large city looking out of the window. The surface of the loch was turned to molten copper by the lowering sun, the trees beyond etched against a sky of cobalt blue.

It was achingly lovely. Gina wished she had someone here to share it with. Not Paul in particular; he had little appreciation of the countryside as such.

She should telephone him, she supposed, yet she felt reluctant. The call he had made to Nick still rankled with her. She was capable of sorting out her own affairs without his intervention. The sooner he grasped that fact, the better for them both.

Around seven-thirty, she called a local taxi company and arranged to be picked up at eight and taken into Callander. There were sure to be plenty of places open where she could get a meal at this time of the year. Pubs were often the best bet.

In casual mood, she chose to wear white trousers and a deep blue silk shirt, fastening back her hair with a matching scarf and treading into low-heeled pumps.

The taxi-driver proved to be young and friendly and more than prepared to recommend a good place at which to eat. He dropped her off at a small hotel just outside the town, and offered to call back for her later. Uncertain of what the service might be like in terms of time, Gina told him she would call the company office when she was ready to leave.

Inside, the atmosphere was genuinely old world, with oak beams and exposed stone-work and a couple of huge fireplaces, one of which held a blazing log fire despite the pleasant warmth of the evening outside.

The dining-room was at the rear, and already almost full. Gina was shown to a table set within a booth similar to the one where she and Nick had drunk coffee that very first morning. It seemed, she thought fleetingly, studying the menu, a long time ago, yet it was only two weeks. How was a year going to seem?

She had ordered, and was sipping a pre-dinner sherry while reading a potted history of the hotel printed on the table mats when someone paused at her elbow. Thinking it the waiter returned in double-quick time with her first course, she looked up with a smile, the latter fading abruptly on realisation.

The man standing there was smiling himself, although his companion certainly wasn't. Fiona looked, Gina thought, like a cat about to be robbed of the cream.

'Would you mind if we shared your table?' asked Nick easily. 'Seems I miscalculated. I should have reserved.'

It was putting her in a cleft stick, came the wry reflection. With three empty places staring her in the face, she could hardly refuse. That Fiona herself would infinitely prefer to find room elsewhere was only too apparent from the look on her face.

A spark of pure devilment sprang to Gina's aid. It would be almost worth it!

'Feel free,' she invited.

'Thanks.' He stood back to allow Fiona to slide along the bench seat before him, pinning her into the corner as he sat down himself right opposite Gina.

He was dressed as casually as she was, in trousers and shirt, unlike his companion who was wearing a suit of cream wild silk more in harmony with a wedding, Gina privately thought, than an evening meal in a pub! Wildly expensive, for sure. Which assessment elicited speculation as to just how much Nick was paying the woman.

'Why the Lone Ranger act?' Nick asked now. 'There's plenty of company back at the ranch.'

'Most of it on a tight rein,' she responded lightly. 'Anyway, I felt like seeing the outside world again.'

'You've barely seen a fraction of the inside one yet,' he came back. 'I'll show you the rest tomorrow.'

Aware of Fiona's reaction, Gina said blandly, 'Will that be before or after our judo session?'

'After—unless you want to get up at the crack of dawn.' If Nick registered the hostility fairly crackling across the table from the woman at his side, he wasn't revealing it. 'Sunday's usually a light day.'

'I thought we were supposed to be going up to Killin,' said Fiona.

'In the afternoon,' he agreed. 'I'm talking about the morning. What would you like to drink?'

Her smile came slow and meaningful. 'I'll have my usual.'

A declaration of intimacy purely for her benefit, Gina surmised. Not that she needed to bother emphasising her claim. Nick was all hers.

As evenings went, this one, by her standards at least, was not a success. Of the three of them, only Nick seemed totally unaware of any atmosphere. He talked mostly about the problems he and her father had met with during the initial stages of the partnership, boring Fiona into the ground to judge from her expression, Gina thought. For herself, she found the whole subject absorbing. Business was business in whatever sphere. Much of what she was hearing might stand her in good stead when her turn came round.

The food proved excellent, the wine Nick insisted on ordering for them all equally so. He drank sparingly himself, Gina noted. That no doubt meant he was driving.

Calling a taxi for herself when the time came to leave was going to prove embarrassing because he would probably feel obliged to drive her back to Langhill before continuing with further plans for the evening. She wondered whether those plans might extend over the whole night, dismissing the thought abruptly as none of her affair. She didn't want to know how far the relationship between him and Fiona actually went.

She was proved correct in her assessment on attempting to beat a retreat via taxi. Nick refused to hear of it. Short of simply walking out on the two of them, Gina had little recourse but to go along with his declared intention of driving her back to Langhill himself. That Fiona didn't like it was only too apparent from the look on her face, only there was little she could do about that either, without showing herself in a bad light.

The realisation that Fiona actually lived close to Callander itself came as a complete surprise. The other gave every indication of dissatisfaction when Nick dropped her off outside the imposingly large house set within its own grounds a mile or so the other side of the little township.

Invited to move up front when he returned to the car after seeing Fiona to the door, Gina could find no adequate reason to refuse. She waited until they were out on the road again and heading back towards the town before making any comment.

'I hope I'm not spoiling anything for you,' she said blandly.

'Fiona lives with her parents,' Nick replied without any specific inflexion.

Gina digested this in silence for a moment. When she spoke again she kept her tone casual. 'I'd have thought her the independent type.'

He shrugged. 'There's a shortage of suitable property available in the area for a single person.'

Gina slanted a brief glance at the hard-hewn profile. 'What about Langhill itself? Wouldn't it be handy having your PA on tap, so to speak?'

'Space is at a premium.'

'There would have been my room going spare if you hadn't talked me into moving in.'

'So there would.' There was a hint of mockery in the agreement. 'Immaterial under the circumstances, isn't it? You're here, Fiona isn't. Why such abiding interest, anyway?'

Gina summoned a shrug of her own. 'I'd hate to think I'd ruined any plans she might have had for taking over tenancy.'

'Like hell you would!' This time the mockery was unconcealed. 'There's something about her that really bugs you. That was more than obvious tonight. You wouldn't, by any chance, be jealous?'

Her laugh was forced. 'I never found need to be jealous of anyone else's looks, thanks!'

'Not what I meant, as you well know.' The pause held deliberation. 'I thought you might resent my interest in her as a woman.'

'Why on earth should I do that?'

The strong mouth tilted at the corner in the way she was beginning to know and dread. 'Just a notion.'

'Totally without foundation, I can assure you!' Gina was too intent on making her lack of interest clear to remember the old adage about protesting too much. 'You may consider yourself God's answer to every maiden's prayer, but my tastes run along very different lines!'

'Such as Paul Milton?' He shook his head. 'I doubt if he's got what it's going to take to handle you the way you need to be handled.'

'You'd have no idea of my needs!' She almost spat the words at him. 'I'm not one of those female masochists who get a thrill out of the big strong man act! If you want the truth, I find your kind of attitude totally nauseating!'

'Sure you do.' His amusement was open and infuriating. 'You know, you'd find life easier if you didn't take it quite so seriously. Loosen up a little.'

The taunt maddened her the more for its closeness to the truth. She *was* taking this whole thing far too seriously. Nick was playing with her; the swifter she was to rise, the better he enjoyed it. The best way to react was to play him at his own game, only that was beyond her at the moment. She felt too stirred up, and not just with anger.

The sudden slowing down of the car to come to a halt at the roadside brought her heart leaping into her throat. It was so dark out here. Even the moon was hidden behind a cloud.

'This might help,' he said, and drew her towards him, hands sliding around her neck beneath the heavy rope of her hair to cup the back of her head as he kissed her.

In those first tumultuous moments, Gina couldn't find it in herself to resist. She had wondered what that mouth of his would feel like, and now she was finding out. Not tender by any means, but not brutal either, persuading her lips to open, to answer, to move against his with growing fervour until realisation dawned.

It cost her a supreme effort to tear herself free of him. Shrinking back into her corner of the car, she attempted to regain some control over her racing pulses. The game had gone too far!

Nick made no move to touch her again. He sat with body half turned towards her, an arm resting across the wheel. His face was shadowed.

'Not quite as repressed as I'd imagined,' he said on an odd note. 'Why the withdrawal? You wanted that as much as I did.'

'I was taken by surprise...' she began, and let the words trail away as she saw his slow smile.

'That's what they call putting the cart before the horse.'

'Stop it!' Her voice had a shake in it. 'If you're feeling deprived, you're at liberty to drop me off and go back to your lady love. Only don't imagine you're going to use me as a stand-in!'

The smile vanished, giving way to a sudden and dangerous tautening of the jawline. When he spoke there was no trace of humour left. 'If that was the intention, I'd have waited until we were outside your bedroom door before making a move. Is it me you don't trust, or yourself?'

Gina slid both hands up her arms in an involuntary hugging movement any psychologist would have recognised as self-protective. 'I wouldn't trust you any further than I could throw you!' she got out. 'You use people to your own ends. For all I know, that included my father too.'

She knew as soon as she had said it that she had gone too far, only it was too late by then to retract. Choosing that moment to slide from behind the cloud, the moon highlighted a warning glitter in the grey eyes as he gazed at her.

'I'll grant you one thing,' he said hardily. 'You know how to put the dagger in. For the record, your father and I had an excellent relationship. He was one of the few people I ever respected, both as a partner and as a friend. I don't really care whether you believe that or not, just so long as you keep your thoughts to yourself in future. Next time you accuse me of something you know nothing about, you're going to regret it.'

No more than she regretted saying it in the first place, Gina thought painfully as he started the car up again. It had been unforgivable. Whatever his faults, Nick was no swindler. She wanted to apologise, but the words wouldn't come. He probably wouldn't be prepared to listen anyway.

They reached Langhill in a silence broken only by the sound of the engine. It was just coming up to eleven-thirty when they went indoors, and one or two people still lingered on the premises. Nick made small talk with a couple seated over coffee close by the stairs, leaving Gina to go up alone.

She was still only halfway up the second flight when he caught her up. His energy, even at this hour, was boundless, she acknowledged. For herself, she felt dull and listless, as if she might be coming down with a cold or something.

'I'm sorry,' she proffered before he could speak— if he'd been going to speak, that was. 'I shouldn't have said what I did back there.'

'Forget it,' he advised a trifle brusquely. 'We all go over the top at times.'

Not him, she thought. He would always be in total command of himself. He had been all of that when he had kissed her. She was the one knocked sideways by the experience. An unprecedented response on her part. Certainly Paul had never managed to arouse that degree of ardour.

Her room was reached first along the landing. Hand on the knob, she said, 'Goodnight.'

'Seven o'clock,' he reminded her, bringing her head round to look at him.

'Is it still on?'

One brow arched in familiar and suddenly no longer quite so irritating fashion. 'Any reason why not?'

'No,' she hastened to deny. 'Seven o'clock it is.'

'We'll cool off with a swim after, so bring a suit.' He was moving on as he spoke, tall and dark and vital. 'Sleep well.'

In her room with the door closed, Gina was conscious of the fact that he was right on the other side of the wall. The thickness of the latter shut out all sound, but she could imagine him moving around: kicking off his shoes, unbuttoning his shirt, stripping off to reveal that broad muscular chest with its dark whorls of hair.

She moistened lips gone suddenly dry, and shut out the intruding images. There was no future in allowing Nick Calway to penetrate her defences.

CHAPTER FIVE

Up at six, Gina spent much of the following hour doing limbering exercises. She had slept, but it hadn't refreshed her as it should.

Today she would have to contact Paul. He was, after all, the man she was eventually going to marry. The fact that at present she felt no interest in marrying anyone was neither here nor there. Everything would be all right again once she saw him face to face.

The side-door to the centre was unlocked. She found Nick waiting for her in the gymnasium with the mats already laid. He was wearing a standard judogi in the newer and finer, if no less strong, material, the black belt about his waist proclaiming his status. Barefoot, he still managed to retain his air of command.

'Right on time,' he acknowledged approvingly. 'I got a judogi out for you, although you'll have to make do with the novice's belt for now. The changing-rooms are right over there.'

There were just two of the latter—both communal. Gina slid out of her jeans and light sweater and took off her lacy brassière too for more freedom of movement before donning the freshly laundered judogi. The familiar feel of the garments was a boost to her confidence.

While not considering herself as in any way Nick's equal when it came to the sport, she was capable of putting up a good enough show to keep him alert. The beauty of judo was that it didn't depend on size, although it was advisable for a woman to go for a throw rather than a grapple when in combat against a man, owing to the difference in weight and brute strength. Pinning someone like Nick to the mat for the statutory thirty seconds was hardly feasible.

He was sitting cross-legged on the far corner of the mat when she went through. Hands resting on bent knees, eyes closed, he looked totally relaxed. Studying him, Gina was aware of tension building inside—of a sudden urge to cancel the coming bout and get the hell away from him before more damage was done.

'Ready?' he asked without opening his eyes. 'Or did you want a little time to gather yourself?'

'I'm fine.' The words came out sharper than she had intended. She modified her tone to add, 'I've already warmed up.'

Nick came to his feet in one smooth lithe movement. The grey eyes were devoid of mockery as he stepped forward to meet her at the centre of the mat. The formal bow came easily to them both, followed by an instant switch into competitive mode, each of them looking for an opening as they slowly circled.

Gina made the first serious attack, grasping the material of his jacket in one hand to yank him off balance while rotating her body to bring him across her hip. Only it didn't work that way, because she was the one who found herself thudding down on to the padded surface, to lie for a brief moment in stunned appreciation of his sheer speed and ability to turn her own movements against her. Not that she could expect anything else from a third dan.

'You OK?' he asked, looming over her.

She got up immediately, ignoring the twinge in her elbow. Bruises were an inevitable part of the sport. 'Just realising what I'm up against,' she said lightly. 'You're really fast!'

He regarded her for a moment with curious expression. 'Would you like me to tone it down?'

'No way!' Her tone was emphatic. 'Where would the challenge be in that?'

'Just a thought.' His eyes narrowed to her face with a look she found distinctly disturbing. 'So let's get to it.'

Get to it they did. Over the following ten minutes or so, Gina lost count of the number of falls she took. She managed to get through Nick's guard just three times, and one of those was more fluke than technique. All the same, she felt a small glow of satisfaction that she was managing to keep her end up. He might win on points, but he wouldn't beat her down. She could keep going as long as he could.

His sudden switch from throwing technique to grappling took her totally by surprise. Pinned flat to the mat by the pressure of both hands on her shoulders, she gazed up into his face with slowly widening eyes as she read the intention in his— feeling the adrenalin surge through her veins for a totally different reason.

He let his weight down on to her by degrees, mouth seeking hers. Nothing she had ever experienced before had prepared her for the swiftness and sheer power of her response. It was like having a fire lit inside her, flames leaping high and fierce and unstoppable.

She kissed him back hungrily, wantonly, lips opening, tongue touching, tasting. The emotive male scent of him filled her nostrils, stimulating her beyond reason. She felt the hard heat of him, the building pressure, and found her hips beginning to move in sensual invitation.

It was only when she felt the touch of his hand at her breast that she realised her jacket had come open. The tingling pleasure aroused was intoxicating. She heard the tiny involuntary moans drawn from her throat as he lowered his head to slide the tip of his tongue over her taut and tender nipple. The sensation was exquisite; close to pain. She didn't want it to stop, yet she could barely stand it to go on either.

It was Nick himself who called a halt. Breath coming harshly, he pressed himself suddenly upright, pulling the material of her jacket across to hide her semi-nudity.

'That,' he said, 'came close to getting out of hand.'

Gina smothered the words trembling on her lips. It was obvious that he had never originally intended the gesture to be any more than another teasing interlude. That it had gone further was as much her fault as his. For a moment or two back there she had been ready to do almost anything he asked of her.

She made a supreme effort to regain some control over her turbulent emotions. Last night had been enough of a give-away. She couldn't afford to have him realise just how far she had come from there. Her voice came out surprisingly steady.

'Do you always finish off a session this way?'

His smile was faint. 'Only with the women. You put up quite a battle. We'll have to have another bout some time.'

Not if she had anything to do with it, Gina thought hollowly. She could still feel the pressure of his lips on her skin; would she ever be able to forget it? Her whole body ached with the need he had aroused so swiftly and easily. Making love with a man like Nick would be a necessity of life. If Paul had been able to rouse even a tenth of the emotions just experienced, they would have been lovers long ago.

She accepted the hand Nick held out to assist her to her feet because to refuse would have been too revealing. He kept hold of it for a moment, forcing her to look at him directly.

'That wasn't planned,' he said. 'Not consciously, anyway. I had this sudden overwhelming urge.'

Her heart jerked, and she could feel the heat rising under her skin. If he was trying to disconcert her all over again, he was succeeding. 'Hardly overwhelming,' she heard herself saying, 'or you wouldn't have stopped when you did.'

His expression altered. 'Is that a complaint?'

Gina made herself laugh and shake her head. 'Just an observation. You said I needed to lighten up.' She turned away. 'What about that swim? It's already twenty to eight.'

'How time passes.' Nick made no attempt to detain her as she stepped past him. 'See you at the pool.'

Changing from judogi to swim-suit took barely moments. Once her luggage arrived she would have a choice of sports-wear, but for the present she had to content herself with the same turquoise and white stripe. Unimportant, anyway, she reflected. She wasn't out to make any further impression.

Whether Nick had been serious in his declaration she still wasn't sure. It didn't really make any difference, as she had no intention of allowing him that close again. She dared not, she acknowledged wryly. Not after the way she had responded. If Nick made love to her at all it would be on the basis of no commitment, and she lacked the ability to be objective about it herself. She knew that already. Better by far to steer well clear. That way she didn't get hurt.

Rob had arrived and was indulging in a brief work-out when she went through to the gymnasium again. He took a break to say a smiling good morning.

'I thought Nick and I were the only early birds around,' he remarked. 'We should get together this morning over the time-table. Can't have classes clashing, can we?'

'Right after breakfast,' Gina promised. 'I'd like to get the times posted on the board before lunch so that people have chance to organise themselves. I'm planning on holding individual sessions if required, to work out diet et cetera. It would be nice to send people home with the incentive to carry on the good work.'

'True.' Rob sounded full of enthusiasm. 'You'll be having some locals on a regular basis too. Deirdre Andrews tells me you're considering evening sessions for those who can't make it during the day.'

'It's a distinct possibility.' Gina glanced up at the big white wall-clock and decided it was too late now to join Nick at the pool. Another five minutes and the main doors would be opened. It was almost a relief to have the decision taken from her hands. Swimming alone with Nick could hardly be calculated as keeping him at arm's length. From now on, she would make sure others were always around.

Showered, and dressed in a green and white print skirt and blouse, she was downstairs for breakfast before the half hour struck. Nick was already seated. He looked at her with enigmatic expression.

'Change your mind?'

'I got talking to Rob,' Gina acknowledged. 'Then it was too late. We're going to spend the morning going over arrangements ready for a start tomorrow. First class ten o'clock on the dot. I'm taking it that I'll be able to utilise the tape-deck from upstairs?'

She was talking too fast and saying too much, but silence would give her too much time to dwell on what had happened less than an hour ago. Sitting there in the T-shirt and jeans he favoured for casual wear, he was no less of a threat to her peace of mind. Those bronzed and muscular arms had held her close and yielding, the long, clever fingers traced intimate patterns over her bare flesh. She found it difficult to stem the hunger inside her for more of the same.

'Have you talked to the boyfriend yet?' he asked unexpectedly.

'No,' she said, and then on a shorter note, 'And don't call him that!'

'Isn't that what he is? You're not engaged.'

'It isn't essential to have a ring to show off to be engaged,' she retorted. 'The understanding is the main thing.'

'And that's what the two of you have?' Nick's tone was dry. 'I'd say he's probably as close to understanding you as I am to breaking the three-minute mile.'

'While you do, I suppose?' The words were dragged from her.

'Better than many, maybe.'

Gina drew in a steadying breath. 'I've been here less than forty-eight hours. Only an egotist could claim to know another person through and through in that time.'

'I didn't say know,' he came back, 'only understand.'

'Aren't they the same thing?'

'Not at all. You can understand what makes an engine work the way it does without knowing every component part. Your engine needs the kind of servicing I doubt this Paul character can provide.'

It was impossible to tell from his expression whether he was mocking her or not. She chose to believe the former for the simple reason that it was safer.

'You must find a facile tongue a real asset when it comes to chatting up the female clientele,' she said with asperity. 'Only don't bother wasting it on me.'

His laugh seemed to confirm her guess. 'I never waste anything. Have some coffee while you're waiting. There's plenty for two.'

Gina took up the offer. She needed something to do with her hands. Nick had been playing with her all along. He still was to a great extent. She had to teach herself to stay inviolate to anything he said or did. It was the only way she was going to be able to live here.

There were only two other tables occupied at present. Breakfast was one meal most people chose to eat in their own quarters. The American couple were right next door. Catching Gina's eye, Mrs Graham gave her a cheery wave.

'Had a real good time last night!' she enthused. 'Didn't we just, Hal?'

'Great!' agreed her husband. 'Nice friendly crowd.'

'I'm so glad you're enjoying your stay at Langhill.' Gina glanced across at Nick. 'This is Nicholas Calway, the owner. The Grahams are from Seattle.'

Nick made a suitably pleasant response to the introduction, but showed no inclination towards furthering a conversation.

'Part owner,' he corrected quietly when the Grahams had turned back to their meal. 'Don't sell yourself short.'

'I've no intention,' she said. 'But there's no need to trot it out to all and sundry.' She lifted her coffee-cup, and added levelly, 'Anyway, it will be all yours in twelve months.'

He looked back at her steadily. 'The offer was to back you after twelve months, not buy you out. It still stands that way.'

'Why?' she demanded. 'What real difference is another year going to make in the end?'

'It was what Martin wanted. The day you reach twenty-five you'll be in a position to govern your own finances, not before.'

Gina gazed at him in sudden and devastating realisation. 'You're telling me you'll want a say in any business I set up before then? That wasn't the arrangement.'

'It was the intention. If you read more into it than that I'm sorry.'

'Oh, sure!' Her tone was biting. 'I can see you're positively dripping in apology! What freedom of choice am I going to have with *you* on my back?'

Firm lips twitched. 'You might like to re-phrase that.'

'Damn you, Nick!' She was too angry to see any humour in the situation. 'And damn your offer too! I'll go back to my original plan.'

'Start sounding out the banks again, you mean?' His shrug invited her to try. 'You'll have to find somewhere to live, of course. "No fixed abode" is hardly likely to impress as an address. And then there's living expenses. Unless you've something put by for a rainy day, that is?'

Gina replaced her cup in its saucer with careful control, crumpling her napkin on to the table as she pushed back her chair prior to getting up. If she didn't get out of here now she was going to throw something at that uncaring, inflexible face.

'Try walking out,' he invited without raising his voice one iota, 'and I'll fetch you right back. That's going to impress our American guests no end.'

The American couple were already casting sideways glances, as if aware of some contention at the next table. Gina forced herself to relax—to sink her pride and give way to a threat she knew would be carried out.

'I despise you!' she hissed across the table.

The shrug came again. 'You'll get over it. If you decide to go back south I can't stop you, but I'd think long and hard about it if I were you.'

He had her hog-tied, and he knew it, Gina thought furiously. There was no way she could manage to set up a business from her present position. Whatever attraction she might have felt for him, it had flown. She had never hated anyone as much as she did Nick Calway at this moment in time.

She ate a breakfast of toast and marmalade without tasting a thing. Nick himself went for the full works with an enjoyment that totally ignored the icy atmosphere. It was almost nine-fifteen when Gina finally made a move.

'I'll be across at the gym,' she said tautly. 'Hopefully, you'll refrain from interfering with my programme in that sphere.'

'I'm not genned up on aerobics,' he returned without rancour. 'It's entirely your baby.'

'Easy to tell you've spent time in America,' she sneered, immediately regretting the remark as his mouth widened into a genuine grin.

'Point taken. I'll watch the vocabulary. Have a nice day!'

He'd won that round too, Gina conceded reluctantly as she left the room. When it came to scoring verbal points, she was no match.

The knowledge of how she had been duped kept her seething all the way across to the gym. She took a moment to calm down before going to join Rob. There was no reason to broadcast the friction between her and Nick. So far as anyone else was concerned she was here because she wanted to be, not because she had been forced.

The following couple of hours spent planning the time-table put her back on even keel again. Leaving Nick aside, she was going to enjoy these coming months. Winters were likely to be less busy, of course, but the local clientele would keep things going at a steady pace. A session of aerobics followed by a feminine get-together over a snack in the bar upstairs would be a big draw for a lot of the wives with children at school and no outside jobs to occupy their minds, Rob declared. A form of therapy.

The message came over the PA system at eleven-thirty. Would Miss Sutherland take a telephone call in the main office?

It could only be Paul, Gina knew. Guilt tempted her to ignore the summons and ring him back herself a little later. It was only the difficulty in explaining her reluctance to answer the call to Rob that despatched her on her way.

Fiona was at her desk, the receiver laid ready beside her. 'He's been hanging on for at least ten minutes,' she said in loud enough tones for the caller to hear every word. 'Long distance too.'

Gina said a cool 'Thanks,' and picked up the instrument. It was obvious that Fiona had no intention of moving from the office while she took the call. The woman was making a show of having work to do regardless of interruptions.

Paul greeted her with acrimony. He'd been waiting in for her call all weekend, he declared. Was it too much to expect that she let him know how things were going?

Conscious of listening ears, Gina made stilted apologies. 'I planned on calling you this afternoon,' she declared. 'It's been a bit hectic.'

'Doing what? You surely haven't started work already?'

'Not exactly. It needed planning though.'

'That took you two days?' The sarcasm cracked. 'What about the evenings? Were they hectic too?'

Gina curbed her inclination to answer him in kind. 'Not so you'd notice. I don't have a telephone in my room, that's all.' She made a valiant effort to put things back on a normal footing. 'Are you still OK for the end of the month?'

'That's what I'm ringing about,' he said. 'Apart from making sure you arrived there at all, that is.' Receiving no reply to this last, he added abruptly, 'I managed to arrange a couple of days off next week, so I'll be coming up on Saturday until the following Tuesday.' He waited for some response, voice taking on a new note when she failed to make it. 'Anything wrong with that?'

Gina shook herself. 'Of course not. I was just ... surprised, that's all. What time do you plan on being here?'

'We can discuss the details later,' he said. 'This call has already cost a small fortune. Phone me tomorrow evening at home.' There was a pause, a seemingly deliberated alteration in mood. 'I miss you, Gina. It just isn't the same here without you.'

'Me too.' It was all she could find to say. 'Bye, Paul. Talk to you tomorrow.'

Replacing the receiver, she met Fiona's eyes over the top of the VDU, at which the latter was supposedly working. The other's smile reached no further than her beautifully painted lips. 'Trouble?' she asked.

Gina answered her automatically, her mind still coping with Paul's announcement. 'Nothing to write home about. Do we have any rooms going spare for next weekend?'

'We can always sort something out.' The smile was still there, yet with a subtle difference. 'How long will your ... friend be coming for?'

'Three nights.' Gina had no intention of responding to the question implied by the meaningful pause. 'Saturday to Tuesday.' It suddenly struck her what day it was. 'Do you often work Sundays?' she asked.

'Only when there's a lot of catching up to do,' came the smooth reply. 'We'll be leaving in an hour or so.'

The 'we' was too emphasised to be missed. She and Nick were driving to a place called Killin this afternoon, Gina recalled. She did her best to ignore the pang at the thought of the two of them together. Fiona was welcome to him.

CHAPTER SIX

BOREDOM was one state of mind unlikely ever to set in at Langhill, Gina acknowledged over the course of the day. Apart from the sports and leisure facilities, the extensive and beautifully landscaped grounds, the wealth of surrounding countryside to explore, there was other entertainment provided several times a week.

It was Rob's suggestion that they join forces to attend the jazz concert which was that evening's contribution. The excellent quartet drew a fair crowd of enthusiasts. The saxophonist in particular was worthy of a professional rather than an amateur career, Gina thought.

It was the first time she had realised that Rob lived on the premises too. He had a room at the back of the centre. His home was in Edinburgh, where he had been employed as a sports master at a comprehensive school until seeing this job advertised in the Press.

'No regrets at all,' he acknowledged when she put the question. 'With one or two exceptions, there's little joy in trying to instil a true competitive spirit in kids mostly interested in seeing who can put the boot in first. I used to spend the school holidays working at a city gym. That helped land me the job here.'

'I doubt if they could have found anyone better qualified,' Gina responded, drawing a smile.

'With you around, I don't need to boost my own ego!'

She laughed and shook her head. 'I don't imagine you go short of feminine admiration. I gather there's no one special in your life at the moment, though.'

'Not to speak of.' He sounded just a little bit withdrawn. 'How about you? Are you serious about this Paul?'

The answer came without conscious prompting. 'I thought I was.' She broke off, dismayed by the admittance. What was she talking about? Of course she was serious about Paul. Nothing had happened to change that. 'I'm feeling a bit cut off, that's all,' she tagged on swiftly. 'Everything will be fine once I see him again.'

'Pity.' The regret was light. 'All the best ones are already taken. I'll just have to make the best of what's left.'

Just noises, Gina told herself with a flash of insight. It wasn't her he was interested in. Not in the emotional sense, at any rate. Whoever it was, she had to be tied up with someone else, hence the remark just made.

Fiona. The name leapt into mind like a bolt from the blue. Why she should be so sure, Gina couldn't have rightfully said, but she was. Not that Rob stood a chance while Nick was around. The Scottish woman had her mind set on becoming Mrs Calway, if she were any judge at all. And that was something *she* preferred not to think about too deeply.

The night was so warm, they went for a stroll in the grounds after the concert finished at ten. The atmosphere between them was companionable, the conversation centred on mutual interests. Gina felt at ease the way she never felt with Nick—the way she doubted she would ever feel with Nick. It was perhaps a good thing that Paul was coming up earlier than anticipated, she thought. She needed some tangible reminder of what she saw in him.

Designed as a replica in miniature of an army assault course, the feature of the grounds which they were making their way towards was laid out parallel with the front drive, though hidden from it by trees. It was intended, Rob said on reaching it, for the older children, but was challenging enough for adults to enjoy it too.

'How about having a go ourselves?' he said, as Gina tested the rope netting forming the first obstacle. 'I've been over it before, so I'll give you a head start.'

The warm night air, the fact that she was wearing trousers and lightweight pumps, plus a reluctance to end the evening and return to her lonely room, all contributed to her unhesitating acceptance. She needed to wind down, and there was no better way than through some form of exercise.

'You're on!' she said, and suited her actions to her words by running up the yielding rungs on all fours.

With safety a priority, the course called for no great feats of gymnastics, but neither was it a walk through. Gina was barely halfway across the rope ladder strung between two poles when she heard Rob mounting the platform at her back.

With only two more obstacles to go, and the moon threatening to vanish any moment behind a cloud, she put on a spurt that fetched her up scarcely two feet ahead of him at the finish line.

Throwing themselves down side by side on the grass, they lay laughing and breathless.

'I think I must be out of condition,' Gina gasped.

'If you are, I am,' said Rob. 'We must have broken several records for speed if not for style. I'll want a return match. Next time with less of a handicap too!'

'Having fun?' enquired an all too familiar voice before Gina could answer, jerking her upright as if pulled by strings.

Nick stood just within the shadow of the nearby trees, hands thrust into trouser pockets. His expression was far from encouraging.

'You have a nasty habit of creeping up on people,' she accused with an asperity born of the need to cover up her involuntary response. 'Yes, we *were* having fun. Isn't that the whole idea?'

'Were we making too much noise?' asked Rob, easing himself a little sheepishly to his feet.

'Enough to wake anyone trying to sleep inside a quarter of a mile radius,' came the clipped retort.

Gina made a derisive sound in her throat. 'Stop exaggerating. It's not even that late!'

'The time,' he said, 'is close on eleven-thirty.'

'Is it really?' Something in her refused to back down and admit he might have a valid point. 'How time passes! Did the Killin trip come up to expectations?'

'I'll say goodnight.' Rob sounded uncomfortable. 'Sorry about the fooling around, Nick. I didn't think.'

The older man nodded. 'See you in the morning.'

'Me too,' said Gina with deliberation. 'Nine-thirty to get things organised. Night, Rob. And thanks for a great evening!'

Still sitting on the grass, she watched him start back in the direction of the house before making any move to get to her feet. Nick offered no assistance.

'You never answered the question,' she said, tucking her shirt back into the top of her trousers. 'How *was* the trip?'

'Fine.' He indicated the drive at his back. 'The car is through there.'

'I'd as soon walk, thanks,' she returned. 'It's hardly going to tax me.'

'You're coming in the car.' He sounded adamant about it. 'I'm not in any mood to argue with you.'

Her hesitation was momentary. Weighed in the balance, it seemed policy to go along with him rather than attempt to put him to any test.

'Frustration can't be easy to live with,' she said with deliberation as she moved to join him. 'I'm surprised you don't find a way round the problem.'

'The only frustration I'm suffering from might be resolved any minute if you don't watch it,' he growled. 'Whose idea was it to try out the assault course at this hour?'

'A joint impulse, if you must know.' She tilted her head to look him straight in the eye, responding to an instinct she couldn't and suddenly didn't want to control. 'Did you never act on impulse?'

It could have been the moonlight that struck the green spark in the greyness, though she doubted it. She made no effort to avoid his grasp, nor to evade his mouth, every nerve-ending in her body alive to the thrill of being in his arms again. It was what she had been wanting all day—what she had been missing since those moments of near surrender in the gym. One could hate a man and still desire him; that much she had discovered.

The shirt she had so recently tucked in came free again to the tug of his hand. His fingers were cool on her breast, and not so gentle. She felt her nipple peak to the erotic stimulation, felt her whole body shudder. She had an almost overwhelming urge to say his name over and over again, to scream it to the heavens in sheer heady ecstasy.

Once again it was Nick who called a halt, except that this time he didn't let go of her right away, drawing back just far enough so that he could see her face. 'What about Paul?'

What about him? was her immediate reaction, swamped by the sudden realisation of what she was doing, and with whom. 'You started it,' she said thickly, trying to find some mitigation in apportioning blame. 'Last night *and* this morning.'

'I know I damned well started it.' His voice was taut, the hand still curving across her collarbone far from tender. He shook his head in apparent rejection. 'This wasn't what Martin had in mind when he asked me to look after your interests.'

'It wasn't what I had in mind when I came here either.' Her voice was husky. 'Can we just forget it?'

Firm lips twisted. 'Put it down to experience, you mean?'

'Something like that.' She was too disgusted with herself to care. One short weekend to bring her to this. What kind of person was she?

'If that's what you want,' he said. 'Let's get up to the house.'

She went with him to the car, and slid into the front passenger-seat. Despite the space between them, he was still too close for comfort. He was wearing light-coloured trousers and matching bomber jacket, his open-necked shirt revealing the strong brown column of his throat. Gina swallowed painfully on the hard lump in her own throat. Forgetting wasn't easy. Not feeling the way she did. She should never have come here at all.

They were at the house inside half a minute. With the bar closed for the night, and most people already retired, the main doors had been locked. Nick had a key. He locked up again behind the two of them.

'You never know who might come wandering round during the night,' he said. 'The gates are purely ornamental. We had to have the whole lower lawn relaid last year after some passing yobbos played midnight football on it.'

He was talking for the sake of it, Gina told herself; trying to put things back on a regular footing. Only it wasn't going to work, because there was nothing regular in this whole situation.

He left her at her bedroom door with a brief 'Goodnight'. Preparing for bed, Gina made a firm resolve to put the weekend aside and start afresh as from morning. She was going to be too busy to spend any time dwelling on things anyway.

For a first aerobics session, the response she received was more than encouraging. Fat, thin and in between, young and not so young, they were all fired by the same aim.

Gina started them off with a few basic movements designed to stimulate without over-exerting. If she did start getting local clients on a regular basis, it might be a good idea to separate the classes in order to provide a more progressive programme, she reflected. There was only a limited amount one could do with those only here for a week or so.

Rob came to watch, shaking his head with a grin when Gina invited him to join in.

'I'll stick to jogging, thanks,' he said. 'It's a grand sight though, ladies!'

Resplendent in a purple leotard and matching leg-warmers, Mrs Graham had been one of the first to sign up. There had only been one other place in their month-long travels where she had been able to indulge her passion for 'body movement', she confided to Gina. This was a bonus indeed!

Aerobics at ten was followed by judo at eleven. Straightening up from the tape-deck where she had been sorting out tapes for the following day, Gina felt her pulse jerk at the sight of Nick coming in through the swing doors from the main gym. He would be wanting to lay out the mats in readiness for his class, of course.

She hadn't seen him at breakfast—whether by intention on his part or not, she wasn't sure—and wasn't fully prepared for facing him now. Last night was still too sharp and clear in her mind for comfort.

The grey eyes registered little as he came towards her. He was already wearing the judogi, making her doubly conscious of the body-moulding brevity of her own leotard. The session just finished hadn't been strenuous enough to make her perspire, thank heaven.

'Everything go OK?' he asked.

'Absolutely fine,' she said. 'They're all coming back again tomorrow—or so they said.'

'Good. You might have to up it to two sessions a day once word gets round.' He paused, and added levelly, 'I understand Paul will be coming up earlier than planned?'

'This next weekend, yes.' She tagged on swiftly, 'Fiona said she'd arrange accommodation. If it's going to be inconvenient...'

'We'll manage,' he said. 'Would you like to give me a hand with the mats?'

She moved to join him at the pile of six-foot by three-foot pads, taking them two at a time to form a large square in the middle of the floor. The plastic side pieces came next. Slotted together, they would hold the mats in position whatever the forces applied.

'Thanks,' Nick said when they were finished. 'Why don't you get into a judogi and join us? I could use you for demonstration.'

Gina stiffened. His tone had been casual enough, but that didn't rule out mockery. The thought that he might have guessed what she was feeling, and found it amusing, stung like acid.

'I don't think so,' she returned shortly.

He made no attempt to persuade her. Leaving him, she went to take a shower and get back into the shorts and sun-top in which she had started the day. Hating Nick was a defence of a kind against other emotions—her only defence. From now on, it had to be that way.

That first week went by more swiftly than Gina had anticipated. By Friday she was up to two sessions a day, with some fanatics attending both. The following week, she promised Deirdre, she would put in a couple of evening classes. The other already had several of Deirdre's friends interested in signing up for a general course of keep-fit.

Whatever attraction Nick might have felt, it appeared to have died a natural death. His manner towards her now was more like that of an elder brother than a man who had declared an overwhelming urge to make love to her. Gina told herself it was all for the best. Even if things had been different, nothing good would have come of it. Fiona was his type of woman.

Paul's arrival on the Saturday afternoon brought mixed feelings. Glad though she was to see him, for once his good looks failed to stir her—a lack more than compensated for by the interest aroused in other female breasts, she acknowledged, wryly aware of Deirdre's reaction on her introducing the two of them. It would be interesting to note Fiona's response that evening.

Nick was out. Where, she had no idea. It had been his suggestion that the four of them patronise the weekend dinner dance. Refusal would, in Gina's estimation, have hinted at reluctance on her part to see him with Fiona outside of office hours. The fact that this was true was neither here nor there.

She took Paul on a tour of the place after tea. He was very much impressed by the whole set-up, and made no secret of it.

'Calway certainly knows what he's about,' he said with somewhat grudging admiration. 'People are always ready to pay top prices for quality. The yearly maintenance fees alone must realise a fair profit, to say nothing of the extras.'

'My father had a hand in it too,' Gina reminded him a little abruptly, and felt his swift glance.

'Well, of course. And now you're here to take his place.'

'Only for a year.' She refrained from mentioning Nick's intention of overseeing any venture into business she attempted at the end of that period. A lot could happen in a year.

Paul seemed about to make some comment, then apparently changed his mind, but there was something in his manner that brought a flicker of doubt to her mind. Imagination, she told herself. Paul knew her plans for the future, and thought the prospects good. Why would he think any differently now?

The room he was to occupy during his stay was a whole landing removed from her own. Parting from him at seven in order to change for dinner, Gina put as much enthusiasm as she could muster into her kiss.

'I'm glad you're here,' she said forcefully.

'So am I,' he responded on a gratified note. 'You really have missed me, haven't you, darling.' It was a statement not a question. 'I'll look forward to continuing this later.'

Thinking about that statement while she showered, Gina wondered just how far he might expect things to go—how far *she* was prepared to let them go, if it came to that. He had come a long way to be with her for such a relatively short time. Surely that deserved a little loosening up on her part? Given any real opportunity, Paul might well prove himself Nick's equal in the arousal stakes.

Dressed in a blue and white flowered cotton dress with a drawstring neckline worn off the shoulder, she added a touch of blue shadow to her eyelids and painted her lips a soft pink to enhance the light tan her skin had acquired over the past week. Her hair she left loose and shining about her face in contrast to the more sophisticated style she was certain Fiona would be sporting tonight. There would be no competing for attention. Not where she was concerned, at any rate. This was going to be a convivial evening.

She had arranged to meet Paul in the bar. Going down at seven-thirty, she found Nick already seated at a table for four.

'Shouldn't the paying customers have first chance of the seats?' she asked lightly, sliding into one opposite him.

'Proprietary privilege,' he returned equally lightly. 'Paul get here OK, did he?'

Gina had little doubt that he already knew the answer to that question, but she answered it anyway. 'Fine, thanks. Had a good day yourself?'

Grey-clad shoulders lifted. 'So-so. I had some business in Glasgow.'

There was no reason to take it that he would have gone alone, Gina reflected. Not that it mattered either way. She stirred restlessly in her seat, aware of the measured scrutiny from across the table, and said hurriedly, 'Fiona's late.'

'*Feminine* privilege.' There was a hint of irony in his tone. 'She'll be here. How about Paul?'

'He's usually the one——' She broke off as the subject under discussion appeared in the doorway, flinging up a hand to attract his attention. 'Over here!'

He threaded his way through the gathering crowd, by no means oblivious to the glances directed his way by the women present. Nick got to his feet to shake hands on Gina's murmured introduction.

Paul was six feet in height, she knew, but Nick still topped him. The latter was broader in the shoulder too, though no heavier in the hip. The seven years or so between them gave Nick the added advantage of maturity. A man into his thirties gained some indefinable quality lacking in the younger element. A kind of inner self-reliance was the closest Gina could come to defining it.

'A fine place you've got here,' declared Paul after drinks had been procured. 'Getting a show like this on the road in only three years calls for real acumen!'

Gina winced inwardly at the clichéd phrasing. Whether Nick thought the same it was impossible to tell. He answered smoothly enough.

'I had help. I understand you're in the catering business yourself.'

Gina was quite sure she hadn't mentioned Paul's job, which meant that Nick had been doing some checking on his own account, though why, she couldn't begin to imagine.

Paul looked a little put out. 'Loosely speaking. My company organises an event from top to bottom. A total service, and second to none!'

'I'm sure.' There was a brief pause before Nick went on levelly, 'Were you planning on joining Gina in her venture?'

'The health club, you mean?' The younger man looked her way, some new expression crossing his face. 'I think that's something we need to discuss.'

'Why?' she asked. 'There was never any question of joining forces before. You don't even have a personal interest in keep-fit.'

'I play squash and badminton regularly,' he protested. 'I'm just not into programmed training, that's all. As to the other, I had every intention of offering you my support, once you got this "going it alone" thing out of your system and accepted that you needed help. Your father's dying altered matters, of course. It hasn't been easy adjusting to losing you for a year, although I understand the reasoning behind the condition.' This last with a glance and a nod of approval back in Nick's direction. 'Time to think things through, eh?'

The shrug was easy. 'Something like that.'

Fiona's arrival cut Gina's intended interjection off at source. Dark hair upswept in a smooth coil, make-up immaculate, she was wearing yet another of the expensive little two-piece outfits, this time in a beige Italian-knit cotton trimmed in white.

'Am I late,' she asked calmly, 'or were you all early?'

'Whichever, it hardly matters,' said Paul before anyone else could speak. He was on his feet, his appraisal of the newcomer openly admiring. 'You'd always be worth waiting for. You're Fiona, of course. Gina said you'd be joining us.' He held out a hand. 'I'm Paul Milton.'

Her answering smile held a warmth Gina had hitherto seen reserved exclusively for Nick. 'Hello, Paul. You're not at all what I expected.'

Leading him to believe she'd been given a misleading impression by yours truly, reflected Gina grimly. Some women would stoop to any low-down trick to show another in a bad light! She stole a glance at Nick to see how he was taking this mutual appreciation society outing, to find him looking at her with an unreadable expression in his eyes. No mockery though, thank heaven. That was one thing she didn't need right now.

She might not have been there for all the notice Paul took of her over the course of the next ten minutes or so. His attention was centred wholly and flatteringly on whatever Fiona happened to be saying, regardless of whether the remark was directed his way or not.

She was lapping it up too. That was apparent from the fleeting, malicious glances she kept winging Gina's way. Nick might be the man she wanted above all others, but that didn't mean she was ready to ignore the rest.

The dinner dance was, as always, well attended. Gina had spent the morning on reception saying goodbye to those leaving, including the American couple. There were still some familiar faces around though, plus a whole new intake, many of whom she hoped to meet first hand on Monday. The twice-weekly evening sessions were to be set aside for the longer-term clients, of which Deirdre was just one already booked.

Paul was the first to suggest a dance, and it was Fiona he asked, not Gina, although he did make the concession of enquiring rhetorically whether Nick minded.

'Entirely up to Fiona,' came the steady reply.

There was some slight hesitation on the Scottish woman's part before she allowed herself to be drawn to her feet. Nick watched the two of them on to the floor, eyes reflective. 'A study in contrasts,' he observed. 'They make a nice pair, don't you think?'

'They could hardly make a trio,' Gina responded shortly, drawing his gaze back to her face.

'Not angry because he asked her first, are you? It's the usual courtesy.'

'I'm not in the least bit angry,' she denied. 'Why on earth should I be?'

He smiled briefly. 'No reason at all. Would *you* like to dance?'

'No!' The refusal came out too strong; she made an effort to temper it. 'Not at the moment, thanks.'

'After dessert then, maybe.' He sounded as if it mattered little to him either way. Fingers curving round his wine-glass, he added, 'You look about sixteen in that get-up.'

Gina made herself meet the grey gaze full on, disregarding the undeniable and ungovernable contraction deep down inside. 'I'm just not the sophisticated type.'

'You're not ingenuous either,' he growled. 'In fact, I'm having difficulty deciding just exactly *what* you are.'

'I'm the girl who's going to marry Paul Milton,' she returned with purpose. 'Just as soon as I get away from this place, that is. If you still insist on having a hand in my business affairs, you'll be dealing with the two of us.'

'Not what you intimated earlier.'

Not what she intended either, came the thought, but there was no reason for him to know that.

The music came to an end, and the group leader announced a short break. Fiona and Paul returned to the table, looking pleased with themselves.

'I've told Paul the next time he comes up he'll have to try some genuine Scottish dancing,' said Fiona, regaining her seat. 'I think he'd pick it up in no time. He's very light on his feet.'

'Pity you won't be here Wednesday,' observed Nick on a casual note. 'We have a team coming in to demonstrate.'

'There'll be other opportunities.' The younger man looked at Gina directly for almost the first time that evening. 'Speaking of which, have you considered how close the set-up here comes to what you were planning in the first place? I think you'd be a fool to let it go for some pipe-dream that might never take off.'

CHAPTER SEVEN

IT TOOK Gina a moment or two to get her mind back into gear after that pronouncement. Nick was the first to respond.

'I take it you'd be prepared to make the move yourself?'

'Naturally.' Paul gave a light laugh. 'Few marriages are likely to work with a partner at each end of the country! I could take some of the load off your shoulders. With Gina's father gone, you must have your work cut out.'

'Dependent on what *I* wanted,' cut in Gina, finding her voice again.

'Of course, darling.' Paul's tone was meant to soothe. 'Only you have to see the sense in it. You'd be starting from scratch in Barchester, and with nothing like the facilities on tap here. Where's the point in taking a risk on a totally new venture when you have one already established?'

'Worth thinking about, maybe.' Nick's voice was level, gaze equally so. 'It's what your father would have wanted.'

'Exactly.' If Paul was at all surprised by the other man's apparent approval of his scheme, he wasn't allowing it to show. 'He wouldn't have left you his share if he hadn't hoped you'd take an active interest in running the business. And consider the other advantages. We'd be able to get married right away instead of waiting. I'd have to give the company time to find a replacement, of course, but a month's notice should suffice.'

He had it all cut and dried, thought Gina dazedly. To have things taken for granted the way Paul was doing was bad enough; to have those selfsame plans openly discussed in front of others far worse. The fact that Nick seemed in agreement with the proposal gave rise to a totally different emotion. It was difficult to believe that he might actually welcome Paul's help in running the estate.

'You could even get married from Langhill,' said Fiona. Her smile was fixed. 'In the absence of your father, Nick could give you away.'

Paul took the suggestion quite seriously. 'Not a bad idea!'

'Not my kind of role, I'm afraid.' Nick spoke easily enough but there was a certain tension in the line of his jaw. 'More wine, Gina?'

She nodded, aware of a betraying quiver deep down as the lean brown hand reached across with the bottle. To stay on here permanently at Langhill in constant sight and sound of this man who could turn her whole world upside down with a single gesture would be foolish—even more so if she married Paul into the bargain.

She wasn't going to marry Paul though. She knew that now for certain. The feelings she had for him didn't go deep enough for any lasting union. How and when she was going to tell him she didn't know, but this certainly was neither the time nor the place.

As if considering that enough had been said for the moment, Paul made no attempt to further the discussion. Watching him as he chatted with Fiona, Gina was struck for the first time by the utter complacency in his manner. He traded on his looks, she thought. Few women were proof against them, and he knew it. She herself was a case in point. Since meeting him she had been mesmerised by the handsome features—flattered by the fact that he had singled her out. Only that wasn't love. Why hadn't she realised it from the first?

The answer was too blindingly obvious. Because she hadn't then met Nick. What she felt for him was far more than just a physical attraction. Since the very first moment she had laid eyes on him she had been fighting to hide from it.

'Dance?' Nick asked quietly as the group struck up again after their short respite, breaking in on her thoughts.

About to refuse, she abruptly changed her mind. Unless she was prepared to give up on everything she had planned, she could hardly spend the next year avoiding any contact at all with him. That there was little possibility of his coming to care for her in the same way she didn't need to be told. His withdrawal this past week had underlined a reluctance to become more deeply involved. That was something she would have to learn to live with.

Fear of betrayal kept her stiff and wooden in his arms when they took to the floor, although every instinct in her cried out to melt against the strong, hard body.

'Relax,' he advised drily after a moment or two. 'I've no intention of doing anything your fiancé might object to.'

He isn't my fiancé, she wanted to say, except that it wasn't the time or place for that either. She owed it to Paul to end the relationship once and for all before he left on Tuesday, only that didn't mean she had to let Nick know immediately too. Allowing him to believe she intended going through with the marriage was her safeguard, if a temporary one, against having him guess just how far and fast she had fallen.

'You looked a bit dropped on back there,' he went on when she made no reply. 'I gathered the idea was news to you too?'

'I hadn't really considered it before,' she acknowledged truthfully. She paused, eyes on the firm mouth too dangerously close. 'It has its merits though.'

'Such as an earlier marriage than anticipated?' His tone was lacking any mocking inflexion.

'That might come into it.' She waited another brief moment before adding, 'You seemed to consider the idea a good one yourself.'

'Staying on here, yes. Marriage...?' He shook his head. 'As I've said before, you're nowhere near ready for it—with anyone.'

'It isn't just anyone I'm considering marrying.'

'So you're only considering it?'

Gina made a hasty adjustment. 'A figure of speech. I could do a lot worse.'

'You don't have to do it at all.'

'You're only saying that,' she countered, 'because you don't really want Paul to have any involvement in Langhill.'

'True enough, I don't.' His tone hardened. 'What's more, I intend seeing that he doesn't.'

Her eyes lifted to meet his. 'How? As my husband, he'd have every right to take a hand if I wanted him to.'

'Living on what?' There was no give in the lean features. 'You're entitled to be taken care of yourself, but I'm still in control of finances. You think he'll be prepared to work for nothing?'

Gina bit her lip. She could tell him the truth, but where would that leave her? Nick was too astute to believe that her volte-face had nothing to do with him. Rather a complete break than have him realise how she really felt. 'You could save us a lot of bother if you just let me have the twenty-five thousand I first asked for,' she said thickly.

'No go.' There was no doubting the obduracy in that statement. 'A year I said, a year I meant.'

'That trust clause might stand up while I was single,' she responded, 'but the courts would possibly take a different view if I were married.'

He gave a small grim smile. 'You could try that angle. I doubt if it would get you far, but who knows? The question is, would Paul be prepared to go along? After all, you could finish up having to wait out the full two years.'

'We'll see,' was all she dared allow herself.

The hand at her back tautened for a moment, then relaxed again. 'Let's do that,' he said.

The others were still talking when they got back to the table. At least, Paul was talking while Fiona listened with flattering attention. She roused herself to give Nick an intimate little smile as he took his seat.

'I thought it might be nice if the four of us took a trip out tomorrow,' she said.

'Fine,' he agreed. 'We can take the steamer across Katrine and walk back, if the weather holds.'

From the expression on Fiona's face, walking had not been the intention, Gina judged, though she rallied swiftly enough. 'Good idea.' Fiona made an issue of checking the time via her watch. 'Sorry to break things up so early, but I think I'll have to be going. I've had a rather long day. Will you see me to the car, Nick?'

This was one night she could be sure of his celibacy, thought Gina, but she took little comfort from the knowledge. Fiona was obviously confident enough of Nick's regard to make arrangements for him without bothering to ask first. That was somehow more telling than any public announcement.

Paul said farewell with evident reluctance. 'A real Scottish beauty,' he declared after the two had departed. 'Totally wasted in the job she's doing here.'

'She doesn't seem to think so,' said Gina tonelessly. 'Perhaps there are compensations.'

'You mean Nick?' He shook his head. 'She's not seriously interested.'

Not admitting it, at any rate, Gina reflected. Aloud she said, 'You and she must have got very cosy if she told you that.'

'I suppose we did,' with a laugh. 'Although I'd quarrel with your choice of word. Fiona and I have a lot in common.'

She kept her voice even. 'More than we have?'

'Of course not.' He studied her indulgently. 'Not jealous, are you?'

He would love it if she were, came the thought. Good for his ego. He was right about Fiona too: they were of a kind. Tomorrow the other would have two admiring men on hand. What better motive for the unexpected invitation?

'No,' she said. 'I have the utmost faith in you.'

A small frown momentarily creased his brow, swiftly clearing as he decided to take the remark at face value. 'That's good. I shouldn't want any misunderstanding between us.'

Especially considering what he hoped to gain from their attachment, Gina figured, and was disturbed by her mounting cynicism. Paul wasn't totally unprincipled; he simply took advantage of opportunity when he saw it. Only not through her.

It was on the tip of her tongue to make her position clear there and then, but she couldn't face it. There was time enough yet. Two more days. After that, she was on her own.

The dinner dance finished at eleven-thirty. Going upstairs, Gina steeled herself for the anticipated goodnight kiss. Paul showed no inclination to pause at the spot where his landing branched off. It was left to her to make the move.

Smile fixed, she said levelly, 'This is where we part company.'

To do him credit, he made no attempt to persuade her otherwise. Shrugging philosophically, he bent to kiss her instead. The small frown was back again when he finally lifted his head.

'Something wrong?' he asked. 'That wasn't the same girl I kissed earlier.'

Gina forced a light response. 'She wasn't as tired as this one. I can hardly keep my eyes open.'

'Not like you,' he said. 'Must be the air up here. Personally, I find it bracing.' He released her with reluctance. 'Best get some sleep, then. We can't have you flaking out tomorrow.'

Fiona wouldn't mind if she cried off, Gina reflected. For a moment she actually contemplated feigning some mild malaise and insisting that Paul go without her, but only for a moment. Spending the day skulking in her room was no answer.

She was up as usual at seven, with time for a morning swim before the pools were opened to the public. Rob was already in the water when she got there. Pausing to watch him as he butterfly-stroked the length of the pool, Gina could only admire his style. By his own admittance, he wasn't fast enough to get anywhere worthwhile in amateur athletics, but that was no detraction.

'I thought you'd have the boyfriend along this morning,' he greeted her when she joined him in the water. 'Isn't he keen?'

'Not at this hour,' Gina admitted. 'Perhaps later, after we get back.'

'Sightseeing, are you?'

'That's right. We're taking the steamer across Loch Katrine with Fiona and Nick.' She was facing him as she spoke, noting the faint contraction of jaw muscle at the pairing of the two names. Another scalp for Fiona to hang at her belt, she thought wryly, though whether the latter knew it or not was open to question. Was she alone in her dislike of the woman, she wondered, or was it simply that, as a female herself, she judged from a wholly different perspective?

'It must be difficult,' he said. 'I mean, you up here and him down there. Doesn't he mind your not seeing each other regularly?'

Doesn't *he* mind, Gina noted, not didn't she? 'We both have our lives to lead,' she responded mildly. 'They just happen to have diverged.'

Rob lifted his shoulders. 'Each to his own. I'd want my girl with me all the time.'

'Then you'd better make sure to choose someone local.' The pause was deliberated. 'Deirdre Andrews isn't spoken for yet, is she?'

'Not that I know of.' Rob gave her a sideways glance. 'Are you matchmaking?'

She laughed. 'Wouldn't dream of it! Show me how to do the butterfly again, will you? I still didn't master the technique.'

There was no sign of Paul when she went back to the house. Showered, and dressed in lemon cotton trousers and sleeveless top, she made her way downstairs to find him already at table with Nick.

'I came along to your room earlier,' he said, 'but you weren't there. I suppose you were out jogging.'

'Swimming,' Gina corrected. 'I jog early evening.'

Taking her seat, she was vitally aware of Nick's dark attraction in the close-fitting white T-shirt. Paul was in casual mode too, although his designer jeans and pale blue shirt were all too obviously band-box new, the neckerchief at his throat a touch theatrical. He looked, Gina thought, as if he had just stepped out from the pages of a magazine.

'A nice morning for a boat ride,' she said a little desperately, for want of any more riveting topic of conversation. 'Is it far to Loch Katrine?'

'Five or six miles,' Nick supplied. 'Ten minutes in the car.'

'The real Trossachs,' declared Paul knowledgeably. 'So many people make the mistake of using the name as a general cover for the whole area. Even you, Gina, when you first mentioned Langhill.'

'Geography was never my strong point,' she said, not about to show any discomfiture over what could only be termed a pedantic observation. 'Is Fiona coming here, or are we picking her up?'

'She's coming here,' Nick acknowledged. 'Callandar is in the opposite direction to where we're going.' He lifted a hand in greeting to a middle-aged couple just entering the dining-room. 'They were our very first clients. They bought four weeks. Two to use here, two to exchange. Most just take the one week.'

'What about the new block of units just completed?' asked Gina.

'Sold out for the whole year, all but a few odd off-peak weeks.' It was Paul who answered, either ignoring or not noticing Nick's ironically lifted eyebrow. 'I'd have thought you'd already know that.'

'Gina doesn't take all that much interest in the financial side of the business,' said the other man. 'Not so far, at any rate.'

Paul laughed. 'I'll be taking enough for us both! I've one or two ideas I'd like to run by you some time.'

Gina held her breath, but Nick answered civilly enough. 'Why not?'

Fiona arrived dressed in a navy and white trouser-suit that made Gina feel like some refugee from the Oxfam shop. Seated at Nick's side in the Rover, the Scottish woman seemed in buoyant mood. Gina made every effort to overcome her own despondency. No one, she vowed, was going to accuse her of putting a damper on the party!

All the same, it was difficult not to feel neglected as Paul followed last night's lead and devoted most of his attention to the passenger up front. Several times she caught Nick's eyes through the driving mirror, but couldn't be sure whether he really was looking at her or at the road behind them. She kept a smile on her face just in case.

A short distance past the lovely wooded little Loch Achray, they entered a rugged pass full of oak and birch and delicate rowan, its steep, over-hanging rocks softened by heather and moss. Pure Rob Roy country, Gina reflected. It would be a wrench to leave all this when the time eventually came. A year from now she would be on the verge of becoming, if not exactly her own boss, at least only semi-dependent. It would be some compensation.

Waiting at the end of a covered wooden jetty, the *Sir Walter Scott* was larger than Gina had antici-pated. Long, low and sparkling white, it had awnings raised over the upper deck, with a single funnel amidships. From here it was possible to see only a small part of the loch, but the sunlit beauty of the surrounding landscape was breathtaking.

There was a fair number of people already on board the steamer, with more arriving by the minute. A chattering, laughing school party in the custody of two teachers who looked very little older than some of their charges brought frowns to a few faces—including, Gina was quick to note, both Fiona's and Paul's. Nick regarded the troop with indulgence.

'Not a job I'd fancy, looking after that little lot for a week or two,' he observed.

'It's disgusting that they're allowed to do that,' said Fiona, eyes on a pre-teens boy and girl with their arms about each other. 'No Scottish school would have it!'

'It's called puppy love,' said Gina, tongue in cheek. 'Something most of us went through at that age.'

Nick grinned. 'And before! I remember a little blonde I was crazy about at nursery school!' Grey eyes rested on Gina's face, the amusement mingled with something else not so easily defined. 'Attraction of opposites, I guess.'

'It's similarities that endure.' Paul sounded a little abrupt. 'What time does this thing leave?'

'Another five minutes,' answered the other man. 'They have coffee and snacks below, if you're interested.'

'Sounds a good idea. How about it, girls?'

'Fine,' agreed Fiona.

Gina shook her head. 'I'd rather stay up here, but the rest of you go, by all means.'

They took her at her word. Gina found herself a seat on one of the benches set facing outwards, and settled down to enjoy the unfolding scene as the steamer pulled out from the jetty and headed for open water around the little headland. One or two people waved from the trail which followed the northern bank. That would be the way they would be returning, Gina assumed.

According to the time-table on display at the booking office, the one-way journey to Stronachlachar at the other end of the loch took forty-five minutes, which had to mean a pretty lengthy walk back. Neither Paul nor Fiona had on footwear designed for any distance.

Someone took seat at her side. She turned her head to smile a friendly greeting, lips stiffening a little when she saw Nick sitting there. 'I thought you were having coffee,' was all she could think of to say.

'Too stuffy down there,' he returned. 'I made my excuses, as they say, and left.' His mouth

stretched into an ironic little smile. 'I doubt if they'll
be far behind, or that I'll have another opportunity
to talk to you on your own, so don't interrupt.' He
paused briefly, eyes holding hers with a suddenly
harder look about them. 'Either you tell Paul to
keep his nose out of things that don't concern him,
or I'll do it for you. I came close to knocking him
through the damned wall this morning!'

He had every cause to resent Paul's assumption
of authority, Gina was bound to acknowledge,
though she had no intention of admitting it. 'That
would have impressed the customers no end,' she
observed, and saw the muscle in his jawline jerk as
his teeth came together.

'The man's nothing but an opportunist. I realise
love is supposed to be blind, but I'd have thought
you had the perception to see that for yourself.'

'Which just goes to show what a rotten judge of
character you are!' She was too angered and hurt
by the taunt to consider her words. 'Whatever I
have will be half Paul's too once we're married—
if we have to fight tooth and nail through the courts
to fix it!'

'That could be a costly exercise.'

'Only to the loser, and we wouldn't lose.'

Mouth set in dangerously compressed lines, he
regarded her reflectively for a long tense moment.
When he spoke it was on a note that sent a sudden
frisson down her spine. 'I'm not going to let you
do it, Gina.'

Her own voice, when she found it, sounded
husky. 'And how would you propose stopping me?'

'That remains to be seen.' His face cleared of
expression as his glance went beyond her. 'Had
enough of the fug down there?'

'More than ready for some fresh air,' agreed Paul, coming into view along with Fiona. 'The coffee wasn't bad, though.' He looked out over the water at the small island passing to starboard. 'Ellen's Isle, isn't it?'

'Eilean Molach, to give it its proper name,' supplied Fiona. She sounded constrained, the glance she shifted from Nick to Gina and back again suspicious. 'The crew are forecasting rain for later on.'

'Not a good omen for our walk back,' said Paul.

Nick stretched out his legs, clasping both hands behind his head in an attitude of total relaxation. 'We shan't be walking back. It was meant as a joke. The loch is nine miles long. I'd have thought you'd already know that.'

Called for, perhaps, Gina thought, but not appreciated by the recipient whose face had taken on a decidedly peeved expression. Right now, that wasn't her main concern. Nick hadn't been joking a moment ago. He had meant every word. Paul was a threat he intended to remove.

She should, she knew, tell him the truth and remove the source of perturbation, but she wasn't ready to do that. If nothing else, his intervention, whatever shape it took, might give her the excuse she needed to break things off with Paul without giving too much away.

CHAPTER EIGHT

PAUL left after breakfast on the Tuesday morning. Watching the car disappear down the drive, Gina acknowledged her cowardice in failing to make the position clear to him before he went. She was left now with a straight choice between letter and telephone call, and fairly soon at that in fairness.

His pride would be the only thing really hurt, she consoled herself. He loved her no more than she loved him when it came right down to it. If this weekend had done nothing else, it had proved that much.

She avoided Nick throughout the day. He had shown little outward reaction to anything Paul had said concerning Langhill since Sunday, nor had he made any attempt to further his declared intention, leading her to believe he had had second thoughts. She didn't see what he could have done, anyway, had her own intention still been to marry Paul. He had no personal jurisdiction.

At six o'clock, dressed in track-suit and trainers, she set off on what had become her regular evening run within the grounds. The jogging track itself was too boringly repetitive in its hundred-metre circuit. She preferred the wooded paths leading up the old folly overlooking the estate.

At this hour there was no one else around, and only birdsong to break the silence. One of the advantages of living this far north, Gina considered, was the stretching of daylight hours during the summer months, although the winter days would of course be that much shorter. Whether she would still be here then she was no longer so sure. It all depended, she thought depressedly, on how far she managed to overcome her feelings for Nick.

Built by the original owner to commemorate some unspecified event, the ornate stone tower at the top of the hill served no useful purpose. It was too dangerously decayed now to climb the stairs leading to the upper chamber, and a new door had been fitted and locked to keep out the unwary.

A wooden seat was set in a sheltered spot on the lee side of the tower, affording the onlooker a fine view of the loch and wooded hills beyond. She was sitting there, considering what she was going to say to Paul, when Nick came round the side of the tower. He was wearing track-suit and trainers too.

'You set a pretty fast pace,' he said.

Gina kept her expression strictly neutral, although her pulses had gone into overdrive. 'I didn't realise you were into jogging,' was all she could find to say.

'I'm not.' He came and took a seat at her side, stretching his legs with a sigh of relief. 'I just used muscles I'd forgotten I had!' There was a pause, a change of tone. 'I followed you up here to talk.'

'About what?'

'Us.'

Her head jerked round, her eyes searching the lean features. 'I'm not sure what you mean.'

He met her gaze steadily. 'It's simple enough. I think if you marry anyone, it should be me.'

It took a moment to actually sink in. Even then she was too stunned to believe the evidence of her own ears. 'What did you say?' she asked weakly.

His mouth twisted. 'You heard.'

The anger pulsing suddenly through her was overwhelming in its force. Anything to safeguard his precious Langhill! Teeth clenched, she said, 'What makes you think I'd even consider marrying *you*?'

'This, for one,' he said, and reached for her.

Resistance ebbed under the calculated assault on her senses. His lips were possessive, compelling response regardless of what her mind was struggling to tell her. He drew her up against him, holding her firmly while he kissed her into a state of total confusion. She could feel his warmth and masculine hardness, and knew that same overpowering desire. No one else could make her feel like this. No one!

Still holding her, he drew back his head to view her face, eyes appraising. 'Not such a bad idea, would you say?' he queried softly.

Recklessness fought a brief battle with caution and lost by a short head. 'It's a ridiculous idea!' she burst out. 'Let go of me, Nick!'

'I like holding you,' he said. 'What's more, I intend to go on doing it until you stop reacting and start thinking seriously about the proposal. You're not in love with Paul. That became more than obvious over the weekend. Even if you were, he's not the man for you.'

'While you are?' She was fighting to retain some semblance of control over a situation fast getting out of hand. 'I'm not in love with you either!'

Something flickered deep down in the grey eyes. 'But you do feel something. I can live with that.'

'Well, I can't!' She tested his hold on her again, desisting only when it became obvious that he had no intention of releasing her. Voice husky, she said, 'This is stupid. You can't marry someone just to stop them from marrying someone else!'

'There's more to it than that,' he said. He brought up a hand to run the ball of his thumb gently over her lips, smiling at the involuntary quiver. 'We both know what.'

'It's still no basis for marriage,' she got out.

'It's a good enough start. Better, I'd go so far as to claim, than you'd enjoy with Paul. He doesn't stir you physically to any great extent, does he?'

She flushed a little. 'How would you know?'

'Observation. His type is too self-interested to be a good lover. It would always be up to *you* to stir *him*. Making love is a shared experience, with both partners making the running.' He added softly, 'You know exactly what I'm talking about. You don't hang back with me.'

'You've probably had a great deal more practice than Paul in eliciting response,' she said with purpose. 'Where exactly does Fiona fit into your plans?'

There was no change of expression. 'She doesn't.'

'Does she know that?'

He shook his head. 'I've given her no reason to believe we had any future together.'

'In other words, you've simply been using her.'

Just for a moment the grey eyes turned steely, then he gave an ironic shrug. 'She's more than capable of making her own decisions. I didn't follow you up here to talk about Fiona. Neither are we going down again until we have things sorted between us.'

'You can't really expect me to do what you're suggesting, just like that,' said Gina desperately.

His arms tautened about her, his mouth set in lines of determination. 'I'm not taking no for an answer, Gina. I won't let Paul have you!'

'You mean you won't let him have any hand in Langhill.' Her voice was thick.

'That comes into it,' he agreed, 'but it's not the be-all and end-all. I've steered clear of marriage up to now only because I hadn't met a woman I could consider living with on a permanent basis. You're a different proposition. The physical aspect aside, I enjoy being with you. From the way you come alive when we're together, I think you get something of a kick out of my company too.'

Something of an understatement, she reflected wryly. Nick stimulated every part of her the way Paul never had and never could. One half of her wanted badly to let him have his way regardless, but the doubts were too strong to be ignored. He hadn't used the one word which would have swayed her. Probably because he wasn't liar enough to pretend to something he didn't and perhaps never would feel.

He was watching her face, assessing her reactions. She stiffened when he drew her to him again, but not for long. She was incapable of resisting that purposeful, knowledgeable mouth. The heat he was generating in her spread throughout her whole body, tingling her skin and turning her limbs to jelly. She found herself pressing closer to him, seeking a contact every inch of her craved for; kissing him back with ever-increasing fervour. There was more to marriage than this, said the small voice of sanity, but it didn't seem to matter all that much at the moment.

There was no thought in her mind of attempting to stop him from pulling down the zip of her track-suit jacket. The thin cotton T-shirt beneath outlined her breasts in thrusting detail. Nick cupped the firm full curves in both hands, his touch inflaming her to a point where she forgot everything else and only wanted him to continue.

Voice roughened, he said, 'There's no point in waiting. I can have a licence in a couple of days.'

It took everything she had to control her instincts and push herself away from him. 'No, Nick! It wouldn't work!'

The sound of voices coming from the far side of the tower gave pause to any move he might have been about to make. Mouth twisting, he said, 'Guess I miscalculated.'

'Yes, you did.' She was on her feet, straightening her clothing with trembling fingers. 'Just leave me alone!'

She left him sitting there, making for one of the other paths down through the trees at a speed far in excess of her normal easy trot. A couple of times she narrowly avoided measuring her length over roots spread across the path, but she kept on going at the same blind pace. Better the risk of a spill than to have Nick catch her up.

Whatever steps she had imagined he might conceivably take, an offer to marry her himself had not been among them. She didn't doubt that he wanted her, but it wasn't enough. She wouldn't allow it to be enough!

She reached the house without mishap. With scarcely half an hour to go before the first of her evening sessions was due to start she needed to pull herself together pretty sharpish, she thought with severity. Forget Nick, forget Paul, forget everything but the job in hand. That was the important thing in her life. From now on, it was going to be the only thing.

With ten regulars among staff and locals already booked, the evening classes looked promising. Deirdre had been one of the first to enrol. She was also the first to arrive. Dressed in purple leotard and matching tights under her coat, she weighed only a couple of pounds over the ideal for her height.

'I'm hoping to get that off tonight,' she admitted. 'And keep it off too. You've no idea how much I've been looking forward to this!'

'Me too,' Gina replied. 'We can work up to some really good routines over the next few weeks.' She looked round with a welcoming smile as the gym doors opened again, feeling her heart give a painful thud before her eyes registered that the man standing there was Rob McKay.

'Thought I might watch you girls at work, if you've no objection,' he said. 'Make a change from the television.' He eyed Deirdre appraisingly. 'Nice outfit.'

'Thanks.' The latter's colour was up, her eyes sparkling. 'Why don't you join in?'

Rob laughed, shaking his head. 'I'll sit this one out.'

He did just that during the course of the following half an hour. A little shy at first of throwing themselves whole-heartedly into the simple routines Gina had worked out for starters, the members soon loosened up and began to enjoy the movements. By the session's end they were one and all eager for more.

'At least come and join us for coffee upstairs,' Gina invited Rob when he showed signs of departure. 'That shouldn't detract from your masculinity too much.'

Her tone drew a surprised glance. 'Hadn't occurred to me that it might,' he acknowledged mildly. 'I thought you ladies might want to talk women talk, that's all.'

Gina made an apologetic gesture. 'Don't mind me. I'm feeling out of sorts.'

'Missing Paul?' he asked with sympathy. 'From what he was telling me yesterday, he'll be up here for good inside a couple of months or so.'

She smiled and shrugged, thankful when he made no attempt to pursue the subject. There would be time enough to let it be known she wasn't going to marry Paul after she had informed him of it. It would let Nick off the hook too.

She made a point of seeing Rob seated beside Deirdre in the cafeteria, and was gratified to find her efforts paying dividends as the two became enmeshed in conversation. Deirdre was so much more his type than Fiona, if only he could see it.

But then the heart and the head didn't always follow the same track, as she knew to her cost.

There was no sign of Nick when she eventually went back to the house at nine-thirty. She washed her hair and dried it before getting ready for bed. Even with the window open, it was too warm tonight for the duvet. She left off her nightdress too and lay between the cool cotton sheets listening to the night sounds drifting in through the window.

Tomorrow she would contact Paul and get it over with, she decided resignedly. Not for his sake but for her own peace of mind. Whether she could bring herself to see out the year was open to question. It wouldn't be easy to keep her feelings under wraps. Her best bet might be to try another appeal for the backing to start up on her own. Under the circumstances, Nick might be prepared to go along this time.

The opening of the door brought her wide awake. With moonlight streaming into the room, there was no mistaking the identity of the intruder. Nick didn't bother to switch on a light but came purposefully across to the bed where she lay clutching the sheet in frozen confusion.

'What do you think you're doing?' she got out. 'I told you to leave me alone!'

'I know what you told me,' he said.

Gina tried to twist away from him as he sat down on the mattress edge, but the sheet wrapped itself about her. Nick turned her back to face him with a hand that was firm but not rough, holding her still to bend and put his lips to hers.

It was impossible to fight the springing emotion; impossible to do anything but go along with him, lips softening, moving, answering the demand he was making on them.

There was a momentary resistance when he freed the sheet and peeled it away from her, but the feel of his hands on her bare skin was too exquisitely pleasurable for the opposition to last. He covered the whole length of her with slow, lingering strokes, building the fire inside her until she could barely contain it; kissing her into a state where time itself ceased to exist.

Her breasts felt full and hot, her nipples taut to the point of pain. She drew an agonised breath when he ran the tip of his tongue over one aching peak before enclosing it fully within his mouth, digging frantic nails into the broad shoulders. Her teeth were clenched, her whole body tensed, yet there was no desire for him to stop what he was doing, only for him to continue, to go further—to do everything and anything he wanted to do with her.

His withdrawal shocked her, made her want to cry out in protest, but he was simply taking the opportunity to remove his clothing. He was fully aroused already, she saw, and felt the tremors start deep down at the thought of what was to come. Too late to turn back, even if he had been prepared to allow it. Not that she wanted to, anyway. She needed to experience that ultimate possession.

He slid down again at her side to begin caressing her once more. His voice was soft, murmuring barely distinguishable words of endearment. Fingers supple, sensitive, he slid a hand slowly and deliciously across the flat plane of her abdomen to infiltrate the silky cluster, parting her trembling thighs to find the very centre of her whole being; causing her to gasp and stiffen for a brief second before her hips began to move of their own accord to the heavy demand.

She clung to him with her fingertips as he moved over her, feeling the heat of him, the vibrant pressure, the intimate intrusion. Pain tore her apart for a fleeting moment, and was gone, leaving her free to answer the rhythmic thrusts, to know the mounting intensity of her own passion until there was no coherent thought left, only sensation.

She cried out when the climax came, not in pain but in sheer rapture. She felt Nick go rigid, heard his breath hiss between his teeth, and was suddenly aware of his weight as he relaxed into her arms. A wonderful sense of achievement stole over her. It had been worth waiting for, worth saving herself for. If Nick wanted her she was his for all time. It didn't even matter at the moment whether he loved her or not.

It was a while before he roused himself to speak. He hadn't withdrawn from her, nor did she want him to. While they were joined like this he was hers.

'You're going to marry me,' he said roughly. 'Say it, Gina!'

'Yes.' The agreement was out before she could stop it—if she had wanted to stop it.

He relaxed again, head coming down on her shoulder. 'Have you any idea what it means to a man to know he's the first?'

'You could tell?'

'Of course.'

She said huskily, 'Because I didn't respond the way I should have?'

His laugh was low. 'You responded magnificently! Experience isn't everything.' He raised his head then, looking down at her with quizzical expression. 'Do I take it you got as much out of it as I did?'

'I suppose.' She could find no more stimulating answer. The moonlight outlined his features clearly, silvering the dark hair at his temples. She felt drowned in love for him. Enough for them both at the moment.

He brought up a hand to stroke her hair with a touch that soothed. 'Like spun gold! I've often wondered how it would look spread across a pillow, and now I know.'

Dark hair would look good that way too, came the thought, hastily discarded before it could do too much harm. 'What will you tell Fiona?' she asked.

He made no attempt at prevarication. 'The truth; what else?'

'You may find you lose your secretary.'

'Then I'll have to get another.' There was a hint of asperity in his tone. 'Forget about Fiona. Where would you like to go for the weekend?'

She looked up at him bemusedly. 'The weekend?'

'A short but hopefully no less romantic honeymoon.' His lips slanted as her expression underwent a change. 'As I said earlier, there's no reason to wait. We can take a longer break later.'

'The whole thing is crazy!' Gina couldn't keep the tremor from her voice. 'Nick, I——'

'You already said yes,' he came back inexorably. 'No backing out now.'

Had she actually said it? she wondered, trying to remember. On the other hand, did it really matter? Crazy or not, she wanted the marriage to go ahead. More than she had ever wanted anything in her life before. It was going to be a shock for Paul—a shock for everyone, if it came to that, but she wasn't going to let that matter either. 'Why so soon though?' she couldn't help asking.

He rolled away from her before answering, lying on his back with one arm entwining hers. 'Because I want it that way. It isn't as if either of us had family on the doorstep.'

'I don't even know if your parents are alive,' she said.

'They were divorced when I was in my early teens. My father lives in France at present; I'm not sure where my mother is.' He sounded matter-of-fact about it. 'I've been on my own for too many years to take them into account.' He reached over to draw her into his arms again, fitting her to the length of his body in a way that caught the breath in her throat. 'It's just the two of us.'

'How do I tell Paul?' she whispered, and felt him go taut for a moment.

'I'll tell him for you.'

And take pleasure in the act, Gina reflected wryly. There had been no love lost between the two men. Would he be in such a hurry to settle matters if she told him there was no question of her ever marrying Paul? she wondered, but couldn't bring herself to put him to the test. His reasons for asking her to marry him might not be all she could have wished, but there was no doubting his desire. It was, as he had said, a start.

CHAPTER NINE

AWAKENING when Nick slid from the bed at dawn, Gina lay still and quiet while he dressed. She kept up the pretence of being asleep when he came back to the bed to look down at her. If he had bent down and kissed her it might have made all the difference, but he didn't.

Only when the door had closed softly behind him did she roll over on to her back to lie gazing unblinkingly at the ceiling while she attempted to straighten out her thoughts. Last night she had been swayed by forces beyond control; in the cold light of day all the doubts returned to plague her.

The speed with which he proposed to effect the marriage was purely on account of Paul, of course. He was taking no chances. If she wanted to be fairer to him than she had been to the former, then she had to tell him the truth and give him the opportunity to think again, even if it did mean losing him.

He was already in the pool when she got there at a quarter to seven. Rob hadn't yet put in an appearance. Diving in, Gina swam underwater to surface at Nick's side in the shallow end where he had stayed to wait for her, fighting a little shy of meeting his eyes with the memory of last night's lovemaking so vivid in her mind.

'Hi,' he greeted her softly as she gained her footing on the tiled bottom. 'I was hoping you'd make it. We have a lot to do today. I propose we go into Stirling first thing and get the arrangements made. We'll need a ring too, of course.'

Gina forced herself to say it. 'It's no go, Nick. Not like this.'

His gaze seemed to harden. 'Why the change of mind?'

'It isn't so much a change of mind as of putting you right,' she said. 'You don't have to marry me to keep Paul away from Langhill. I'd already decided to break things off with him.'

He studied her for a long moment with narrowed intensity. 'That wasn't the impression you gave on Sunday.'

'I know.' She lifted supple shoulders in a wry little shrug. 'I wasn't seeing very straight. You were right—it would never have worked out between Paul and me. I don't feel enough for him.'

'So why let him go away believing it's still on?' Nick's tone was abrupt. 'The time to tell him would have been face to face.'

'I know that too.' She gave another wry shrug. 'So I'm a coward at heart. Anyway, that's something I have to deal with myself. The point is, as I said, you don't have to go to such lengths to secure Langhill any more.'

There was no reading the mind behind the steady regard. 'You don't want marriage?'

'It's too lacking in all the important things,' she said desperately.

'Such as?'

She drew in a shallow breath. 'Such as love, for instance. We've known each other less than a month all told.'

He said levelly. 'Five minutes can be enough. I wanted you the first time I laid eyes on you. I've a fancy you experienced the same, hence the antagonism.'

'That's attraction,' Gina countered, 'not love. It can fade.'

'Or grow into something deeper.'

'Given time, perhaps. Rushing into marriage on the strength of it could be fatal.' She searched the grey eyes, looking for something she knew she wasn't going to find. 'It isn't only that either. I doubt if it would have entered your head at all if you hadn't been intent on keeping Paul out of the picture.'

His lips slanted. 'I can't deny that was a part of it, but the idea still seems a good one. I take it you're not totally against it.'

She said slowly, 'You're suggesting we should still go ahead?'

'Why not? The factors I outlined yesterday still apply. We're compatible in most departments.' Grey eyes took on a look that made her toes curl in memory. 'Very much so.'

The muscles of his thighs braced to support her as he drew her up against him. He held her head still with a hand at her nape while he kissed her long and hard. Helplessly, she began kissing him back, winding her arms about his neck to bring herself even closer into contact. She wanted him so badly she could scarcely contain the need. Whatever he might be lacking in emotional depth, he more than made up for in physical ardour. She couldn't have enough of him.

It took Rob's appearance through the rear door to bring her back to earth. Even then, Nick made no attempt to release her. The younger man halted on sight of them, surprise written large on his face.

'Sorry,' he proffered in some obvious discomfiture. 'I didn't realise...'

'Be the first to congratulate us,' Nick invited smoothly. 'We're getting married.' He stilled Gina's protesting movement, smiling down into her eyes with a look that defied her to try denying it.

Looking thoroughly nonplussed, Rob said blankly, 'I thought Paul was the lucky man.'

'Not any more.' Nick's tone was equitable enough but there was no doubting the resolve. 'Aren't you going to wish us luck?'

'Well, yes.' Rob glanced at Gina as if puzzled by her silence. 'Sorry for the reaction. I just didn't expect...'

Contradiction now could only serve to confuse the issue even more, Gina acknowledged. She was too confused herself to be sure of just *what* she did want. 'It's all right, Rob,' she said as his voice trailed off. 'It's been a surprise for me too.' She drew away from Nick. 'We're just leaving. The pool is all yours.'

Nick hoisted himself up over the edge in her wake, slinging an arm about her shoulders as they moved towards the other man. Gina's smile felt fixed. 'See you later,' she said.

'Do I keep the news to myself?' Rob asked. 'Or is it for general release?'

Nick did the answering. 'It's no secret. Tell who you like.'

Gina waited until they were out of earshot before giving voice. 'You shouldn't have done that. What's everyone going to think?'

'It's nothing to do with anyone else,' he said. 'If the weekend is too soon for you, when would you suggest?'

They had reached the parting of the ways. Gina paused to look at him with uncertainty. 'You really, seriously want this?' she asked.

'Really, seriously,' he repeated with a familiar hint of mockery. 'I'm not in the habit of joking about such things. If I'm going to do it at all I can't think of a better person to do it with. We have everything going for us, Gina.'

Not quite everything, she thought, but she would settle for it anyway. Feeling the way she did about him, what else was there?

'We'll talk about it over breakfast,' he said. 'Go and get dried.'

Food was the last thing on Gina's mind as she towelled herself dry. With the 'if' settled, there still remained the question of 'when?'. First and foremost, Paul had to be told. A daunting task in itself. He wasn't going to accept the rejection easily. More especially so when he heard about Nick.

Then there was her mother, of course. Considering the speed with which her own relationship with Robert had developed, she would surely make allowances. All the same, it might be best to present her with a *fait accompli* rather than telephone the news in advance.

Nick was already at the table when she got there half an hour later. He was wearing the same grey suit he had worn the morning they had visited the solicitor, she noted. Less than four weeks ago. It scarcely seemed possible.

'I've an early appointment,' he said by way of explanation. His smile brought a glow deep down. 'You look fresh as the proverbial daisy—or should I say buttercup?'

'Yellow's my favourite colour,' Gina admitted, touching the collar of her shirt. 'Like sunshine.' She reached for the coffee-pot, adding huskily, 'I have to tell Paul myself. It wouldn't be fair for him to hear it from you.'

The dark head inclined. 'He'll probably be ringing you this morning, considering he didn't get to speak to you last night.'

Her eyes widened. 'He rang last night?'

'While you were across at the centre.'

'Why wasn't I called?'

'Because I gave instructions that you weren't to be interrupted,' came the unequivocal response. 'You could hardly walk out on a class halfway through a routine. It might be an idea to ring him before you go over this morning, for the same reason.'

'He'll be on his way to work by now,' she said. 'I can hardly tell him what I have to tell him there.'

'Tonight, then. Otherwise, I *will* do it for you.'

Gina said softly, 'You can be quite ruthless, can't you?'

'When it comes to something I want,' he agreed. 'You don't have any deep feelings for the man, so it shouldn't be that difficult. Just tell him the truth.'

'And when are *you* going to tell Fiona?' she asked, and saw some fleeting expression cross the lean features.

'At the first reasonable opportunity.'

'She's going to be . . . upset.'

The faintest of smiles touched his lips. 'Does it bother you?'

'Not to any great extent,' she confessed. She hesitated to ask the question foremost in her mind, yet couldn't keep it back. 'Do you...have you slept with her, too?'

The smile disappeared. 'I'm not prepared to go into detail,' he said. 'Either about Fiona or any other woman I might have taken interest in. What's past is past. It's the present that matters now. You and me.'

'Providing it stays that way,' she said with intent.

'As to that,' he returned, 'you'll just have to trust me.' He glanced at his watch and pushed back his chair. 'Time I got going.' On his feet, he paused to look down at her. 'How would you fancy lunch out somewhere? Just the two of us.'

'With champagne to celebrate?' Gina asked lightly, and saw his mouth slant again.

'The best idea yet! Be ready at noon.'

She watched him cross the room to the door, tall, and lithe and devastating. Tonight they would be together again, she thought with a delicious tensing inside. She could hardly wait!

Rob greeted her with restraint when she arrived at the gym. 'That was some surprise you sprang at the pool,' he said. 'Does Paul know?'

Gina made a rueful gesture. 'Not yet. I—It all happened so fast.'

'It must have,' he agreed. 'I didn't think you even liked Nick all that much.'

'Neither did I,' she said. She summoned a smile. 'Seems we were both wrong. I'd better go and get ready.'

Rob wasn't the only one who was going to consider the whole thing odd, she acknowledged as she limbered up with a few stretching exercises. Facing everyone once the news got round wasn't going to be easy. They'd all seen her with Paul over the weekend. She owed none of them explanations, of course, but her apparent change of heart would cause endless speculation. Not that it would matter to Nick. He was inured to outside opinion.

She would have to try cultivating a little of the same attitude, she reflected. To hell with what anyone else thought! All she cared about was Nick.

Fiona was leafing through the second delivery of mail at reception when she went back to the house at eleven-thirty. From the coldness of the other's expression as their glances briefly clashed, Gina gathered that the news had indeed been imparted, which meant that Nick was back.

She wondered what reaction he had received. It would depend, she supposed, on just how far the relationship had gone. She felt no satisfaction. Fiona might not be all sweetness and light, but that wasn't to say she couldn't be hurt. Rejection was rejection, whichever way it was phrased.

The Scottish woman was not in evidence when she came downstairs again on the stroke of twelve. Cool, and outwardly collected in a cream linen suit, she went outside to find Nick standing by the car.

'Right on the dot,' he approved. 'I've just got here myself.' He saw her seated before coming round to slide behind the wheel. 'We're going over to Dunblane.'

'How did Fiona take the news?' Gina asked tentatively as he started the engine and began reversing out of the space.

'How would you expect her to have taken it?' he countered without expression. 'I told her what was happening—end of story.'

'No recriminations?'

'None merited. There was no commitment.'

Not on his side, perhaps, Gina thought, but almost certainly on hers. 'She won't be leaving, then?' she said.

'Not that I know of.' He sounded abrupt. 'Can we forget about Fiona? I take it you haven't spoken to Paul yet.'

She shook her head. 'I left a message with switch that I'd ring him tonight, but I forgot to ask if he'd phoned at all.' She added wryly, 'I'm not at all sure what I'm going to say.'

'Try the plain facts,' Nick suggested drily. 'No point in wrapping it up.'

'He's not going to accept it.'

'He'll have to accept it. He doesn't have any choice.' He paused, glancing her way with narrowed appraisement. 'Having doubts?'

'About Paul?' She shook her head. 'I told you, I'd already decided to end it.'

'About us, then?'

'Some,' she admitted. She repeated what she had said to Rob earlier. 'It's all happened so fast.'

'Paul precipitated it himself. Given time, it would have happened anyway.' His tone lightened. 'You've been giving me restless nights since you got here, plus a whole lot of daily aggravation too. Not good for business.'

Gina kept her tone equally light. 'At least you won't have to buy me out now.'

'A bonus,' he agreed. 'Not that you'll be losing out.'

Only where the deeper emotions were concerned, she thought. She made an effort to cast off the sudden despondency. Half a loaf was better than none at all, especially when it came buttered and jammed to boot.

Standing in extensive landscaped grounds, the hotel to which he took her was littered with paintings and tapestries and antiques. They had a drink in the bar before going in to lunch in the magnificent dining-room.

'This is going to cost the earth,' Gina commented, perusing the menu.

'I think the bank can stand it.' Nick sounded amused. 'Are you going to be a thrifty wife?'

She laughed, aware of the thrill the word alone elicited. 'In true Scottish tradition!'

'Except that you're not Scots.'

'A detail. I don't like paying through the nose, that's all.'

'You won't be,' he pointed out. 'Neither will I. The food here is worth every penny.' He studied the menu himself. 'How about sharing a Chateaubriand?'

'For lunch? I doubt if I could do it justice.'

'What you can't eat I can,' he returned equably. 'Unless you've another preference?'

She shook her head, happy to agree to anything he suggested at the moment. Whether she would always be as amenable remained to be seen. Knowing her own nature, it was doubtful, but total unanimity could become very boring. If Nick had wanted a yes-woman he would have found one.

The promised champagne came served in a bed of ice. Nick raised his glass when the wine-waiter had departed. 'To us,' he said.

'It's bad luck to drink to yourself,' she responded, but she did it anyway, replacing the glass on the table with a sense of having finally and irrevocably committed herself.

Nick took a small box from his pocket and opened it before placing it in front of her, watching her face as she studied the contents. The ring was a diamond cluster set around a square sapphire, the whole thing sparkling in the light from the window behind her. Victorian, and worth a small fortune, Gina judged. She hardly knew what to say.

'Put it on,' Nick invited. 'I had to take a guess at the size, but it can always be altered if necessary.'

She took the ring from the box with fingers gone clumsy, and slid it on.

'Are you being deliberately obtuse?' he asked. 'That's the wrong hand.'

'Sorry,' she said. 'I—I'm not used to wearing rings at all.'

His tone altered. 'My fault. I should have waited till later and put it on for you.' He reached across and performed the exchange with dexterity, heedless of any watching eyes. 'Fits beautifully. How do you like it?'

'It's superb,' Gina acknowledged. She could scarcely have said anything else. 'I just didn't expect it.'

'You're entitled to a formal engagement, no matter how short.' The pause itself was brief. 'Which brings us back to the main point. When? I'd prefer a swift and simple civil ceremony myself, but if you have any strong feelings otherwise I'm prepared to make a concession.'

The only one, she gathered. Well, that suited her too. The last thing she wanted was any fuss-making. 'Whenever you like,' she said recklessly. 'You were right—there's nothing to wait for.'

He smiled. 'I'm glad you feel the same way. How about next Thursday? They were fully booked this weekend after all.'

'What you're saying,' she challenged, 'is that you already arranged it for Thursday before you asked.'

'True.' The grey eyes were unrepentant. 'The earliest I could get. We can use a couple of the staff as witnesses.'

'You mean we don't tell anyone at all?'

'Not unless you want a whole lot of curious on-lookers. We'll be flying over to Paris for a few days right after. Dinner at Maxim's for starters, followed by three nights of wedded bliss.' He spoke lightly enough but the seriousness was there underneath. 'Sound good?'

Gina laughed. 'It sounds out of this world! I've never been to Paris.'

'Not the best time of year to visit,' he advised, 'but I dare say we'll find compensations.'

More than enough, she thought. The days would be fabulous, the nights even more so. Just the two of them together. She could even find room to feel sorry for Fiona, who would never know that particular delight—at least, not with Nick. And afterwards there was Langhill. Home from now on.

'Whose room do we get to share,' she asked, 'assuming that's what we will be doing?'

Nick shook his head. 'Hardly practical. The last of the house apartments was only completed recently, so it hasn't been put on the market yet. We'll have that for the time being. Later, we could possibly build our own place in the grounds. There's space enough.'

He had covered everything, Gina reflected. Nothing left to chance. Except for love, that was.

They got back to Langhill at four to find a message at the desk for Gina to telephone Paul at the earliest opportunity.

'Best get it over with,' Nick advised. 'Use the phone in the sitting-room. I'm going up to change.'

Fiona was in the office. She looked up with a swiftly altering expression on seeing who had entered the room. 'Come to gloat?' she asked.

'I've a phone call to make,' Gina answered, refusing to be drawn.

'Explaining yourself to Paul? That should be fun for you.' She added harshly, 'He's well rid of you. He merits better!'

'So why not offer to console him?' Gina suggested icily, and was instantly contrite. That was rubbing salt into the wounds with a vengeance! 'I'm sorry,' she proffered. 'I shouldn't have said that.'

'Don't let it worry you. It's no more than I'd expect.' Fiona was obviously not about to forgive *or* forget in a hurry. 'You do appreciate just why Nick's doing this, of course? It's called expediency. Martin did him a real disservice in leaving his share of the business to you. This way he at least makes sure no one else gets a look in.'

'There's more to it than that...' Gina began, then caught herself up abruptly as she realised what she was saying. She didn't have to justify herself. Not to Fiona, or anyone else for that matter.

All the same, the comment had hit hard. Ousting Paul was only a temporary measure. Any man she married would constitute a threat.

She had to force herself to look at the thing rationally. So she already knew that Nick didn't feel as much for her as she felt for him, but he wasn't exactly indifferent to her either. She could cope with that. 'I don't want disturbing,' she said coolly, and went on through to the sitting-room.

Paul would still be at the office at this hour. Reluctant as she was to contact him there, she couldn't in all fairness leave it any longer. She put the call through, half hoping he would be otherwise engaged, heart jerking painfully when his voice came over the line.

'Milton here.'

'It's Gina,' she said. 'Paul, I——'

'Where the devil have you been?' he demanded. 'I've been trying to get hold of you since last night!'

'You didn't get my message?' she asked a little lamely. 'I asked switch to tell you I'd phone you tonight.'

'I'm not going to be in tonight,' came the testy response. 'I have things to do other than hanging around waiting for you to deign to call me.'

Such as what? Gina wondered briefly. Or should it be, With whom? She took herself to task at the uncharitable thought. No use trying to justify her own actions by accusing him of any double dealing. There was only one way to say it and that was straight out.

'I can't marry you, Paul.'

The silence was so lengthy she thought they had been cut off. When he did speak it was on a totally altered note.

'What are you talking about? We just spent the whole weekend making plans!'

'*You* spent the weekend making plans,' she said. 'I realise I should have spoken up while you were here, but I . . . well, I just didn't. No excuses. It was wrong to leave it till now, and I'm . . . sorry.'

'It's Nick, isn't it?' The question was clipped. 'What's he been saying to you?'

He was going to find out sooner or later, Gina conceded resignedly, so she might just as well admit it. 'He asked me to marry him,' she said. 'I told him yes.'

'You can't be serious!' Paul sounded stunned. 'Gina, that's ridiculous! You hardly know the man!' He paused, obviously searching for words. 'You realise why he's doing this, don't you? He wants to retain full control.'

'I'll be keeping my own interest,' she responded. 'I do know what I'm doing—believe it.'

'I *don't* believe it. And I certainly don't accept it.' His voice took on a new note. 'I'm not going to let you do this, Gina. I'll be back up there on Saturday!'

'You'll be wasting your time.' She was desperate to convince him. 'I'm sorry I wasn't straight with you, but it's no use. I'm going to marry Nick!'

She replaced the receiver before he could reply, to sit for a moment or two trying to get a hold of herself. He wouldn't really come back. When he stopped to consider, he'd realise it was too late. He *had* to realise it.

CHAPTER TEN

GINA was still sitting there when Nick came into the room. He was back in more casual clothing again.

'All done?' he asked.

'All done,' she said, and hoped she was right. 'I'm ready for a shower myself.'

'Later.' Nick came over to draw her to her feet, setting her senses alight with his possessive touch. His kiss made her ache. 'We didn't get to seal the bargain properly yet,' he said softly.

'I thought we did that last night,' Gina murmured, and tremored again to the slow and sensual smile.

'That was just the aperitif. The main course is still to come.'

'Not here,' she said hastily. 'Fiona is right outside.'

Grey eyes darkened. 'She's hardly going to walk in.'

Who could be sure? she thought. There was no lock on the door. In any case, it wasn't on. She didn't have the ability to ignore the other woman's close presence. Nick was wrong to expect it of her.

He studied her face for a moment, then shrugged and let her go. 'It will keep. Go and get your shower.'

She had disappointed him, Gina knew, but she couldn't help that. She would make it up to him later. The very thought of another night like the last made her weak at the knees. On impulse, she reached up and caught his head between her hands, bringing it down to press her lips to his in pure passionate longing. She loved him so much he *had* to love her back. She was going to do everything in her power to make him love her!

'Don't tease,' he growled when she slid away from him again. 'I'm past playing those kind of games.'

The injustice and hurt of the accusation struck deep, cancelling out everything but the sudden urge to strike back. 'I see,' she said tartly. 'All or nothing! In that case, we'll make it nothing, shall we?'

He caught her up before she reached the door, swinging her about to lift her bodily from the floor and carry her back to the sofa. Dropped on to the cushions, Gina glowered up at him, surprised to see him smiling, albeit faintly.

'There's one thing obvious,' he said. 'I'm going to have to teach you the difference between male and female responses. You might be capable of switching off at the drop of a hat; I'm not. Kiss me the way you just did without following through, and I'm going to react the way *I* just did. It's called human nature. And bed, by the way, isn't the only place to make love.'

'I'm sure you'd know,' she retorted, and wished she hadn't as the smile faded out altogether. 'Sorry,' she said swiftly. 'That wasn't called for.'

Nick shrugged, expression unrevealing. 'Depends on the viewpoint, I suppose.' He moved away. 'I've a couple of calls to make myself. Did you want dinner here or out?'

Gina struggled to find something adequate to say to him—to make him understand her feelings—and

failed miserably. He was right: they had totally dif-
fering viewpoints. Compromise was the obvious
answer, but one not easy to achieve in the circumstances. She was only just beginning to realise how
little she really did know this man she had promised
to marry.

'Here will be fine,' she said stiffly. 'I'll leave you
to it, then.'

He made no answer. Going out, she resisted the
urge to vent her spleen by slamming the door. Not
for anything was she going to give Fiona the
satisfaction of knowing things weren't going quite
so well as it appeared. One way or another, they'd
work it out.

The Scottish woman was clearing her desk in
readiness for departure. She looked withdrawn.
Gina said a civil, 'Goodnight,' and made her
escape.

It would be of some help if Fiona would up and
leave, she reflected wryly, but the woman apparently had no intention. Jobs like this one were too
scarce in the area to throw away, she supposed,
regardless of the cost. Yet Callandar itself could
surely hold little pull now that Nick was out of
reach?

Unless, of course, hope still lived. It depended
on just what Nick *had* told her. His commitment,
after all, was mostly one of expediency. Maybe he
planned on retaining Fiona as a sideline. No doubt
she satisfied him in *every* department!

She had to stop this, Gina told herself hollowly.
'Trust me,' Nick had said. She could at least give
him the chance to prove that she could.

She went jogging as usual at six. Exercise at least
gave her something other to do than sit twiddling

her thumbs and thinking. Just twenty-four hours ago she had been, if not happy, at least reconciled. Now, she wasn't sure where she was. One-sided love was proving harder to support than she had allowed for. Coupled to suspicion, it became nigh on untenable.

Rounding the folly to find Nick already occupying the wooden seat was a shock to her entire system. She came to a sudden halt, to stand looking at him in questioning silence.

'Beat you to it tonight,' he said. 'I might even take this up as a regular thing. Those who run together stay together.'

'You don't have to,' she said. 'Join me, I mean.'

His regard hardened a fraction. 'Is that by way of saying you don't want me to?'

'No, of course not. I simply meant...' She broke off, shaking her head in renunciation. 'Forget it. I'm sick of being misunderstood.'

'Maybe with some reason,' he agreed. 'I played a bad hand earlier. Priorities get confused at times. I'd spent three hours watching you across a table without being able to do more than touch your hand. I guess it all caught up with me once we were on our own.'

Warmth was spreading through her, allaying doubt as it went. This was something she could relate to. 'I didn't handle things very well myself,' she said huskily. 'Don't think I didn't want you, Nick. You've no idea just how much I do!'

Grey eyes took on a softer look. 'I'm willing to be convinced.'

There was no Fiona up here, Gina acknowledged, although the venue still left a lot to be desired. She made herself go to him, sliding down on to his knees to put her lips tentatively to the firmly moulded mouth. If this marriage was going to have any chance at all she had to meet him halfway. He had already made his contribution.

He took it more slowly this time, lips and hands gentle. Gina made no demur when he pulled the zip on her track-suit and freed the bottom of her T-shirt from her trousers to slide warm fingers up inside. She was wearing an elasticated athletics brassière which proved no barrier. His touch made her shiver.

'You're everything a man could want,' he murmured thickly. 'Young and firm and beautiful! Do you know what you do to me?'

She could feel what she was doing to him—feel what he was doing to her. If this wasn't love it was the closest thing to it. Her kisses grew in intensity, mouth eager, seeking a closer, deeper union. His tongue parted her lips with gentle insistence. Gina found herself responding in kind, teasing him into a fiercer, more possessive encroachment. She no longer cared where they were, only that they were together.

There was some long grass nearby. Nick carried her over and laid her down in the middle of it. Her senses were tuned to a degree that made everything more acute. She could hear the rustle of minute creatures in the grass, feel the thudding of her heart, smell the faint musky odour of his skin as she pressed her lips into the dampened hair of his chest.

Smooth, unblemished skin tanned golden brown, taut with muscle over which her fingers moved in delicate surveillance. No single ounce of surplus flesh marred the superb male structure. He was all she had ever admired—all she could ever have asked for. She could only hope that she pleased him as much.

His hands were warm and sure as they slid away the last of her garments. He followed the movement with his mouth, making her gasp and writhe in an ecstasy of sensation. He kissed his way back up the length of her body by slow degrees, gradually lowering himself until she felt the full potent pressure and irresistible demand.

No pain this time. They slid together easily, wonderfully, moving as one in a hunger that became a frenzy. Then everything blurred and fell away.

It was almost seven-thirty when they finally got back to the house. Gina felt as close to contented as she was going to get, considering what was still missing from the relationship. As a lover, Nick left nothing to be desired. She had to count herself lucky to be in the position in which she was. Some women achieved fulfilment in neither sphere.

Standing under the shower, she contemplated the forthcoming wedding, regretting the lack of ceremony about the arrangement. It would have been nice to have *someone* there. Like Deirdre and Rob, for instance. They could have stood witness for them instead of using people they didn't even know.

There was no real reason why it still couldn't be arranged that way, she supposed. It wasn't as if she wanted a whole crowd of people. Nick surely wouldn't mind. Both Deirdre and Rob could be trusted not to spread the date and time around.

Nick put up little resistance to the idea when she mentioned it over dinner.

'If it's what you want,' he said. 'I simply thought it would make things easier if we just slipped away.'

His regard rested on her face for a moment, expression difficult to read. 'Are you missing all the pomp and circumstance usually associated with weddings?'

Gina shook her head. 'As you said, we neither of us have family available, and they're the ones who tend to like a show. I just didn't fancy having nothing but total strangers around.' She smiled. 'Anyway, it might give the two of them some incentive. It's about time Rob realised Deirdre is far more his type than...'

'Than whom?' prompted Nick with mild curiosity as her voice petered out. 'Someone here?'

Too late to start coming up with alternatives, Gina conceded ruefully. She hadn't meant to bring up the name again, but she could hardly leave it there.

'He's keen on Fiona,' she acknowledged.

Nick lifted a well-schooled eyebrow. 'He told you that himself?'

'Not in so many words.'

'I see: feminine intuition at work again. It isn't always reliable.'

'It is in this instance.' She added diffidently, 'Does it bother you?'

'Should it?' he countered. 'I dare say there are a number of men here who fancy Fiona.' His tone had shortened. 'I thought we were going to forget about her.'

Gina looked at him uncertainly for a moment before speaking her mind. 'I'm finding it difficult to do that with her right here under my nose.'

'You're suggesting I terminate her employment?'

Her face warmed, but she stood firm. 'I don't think that's so unreasonable.'

'On what grounds exactly?' There was irony in the question. 'The law requires adequate cause.'

'You're saying she'd take you to court?'

'She might. That's not the whole issue though.'

'So what is?' she challenged, and saw the glint of impatience in his eyes.

'The fact that I'm unlikely to find another secretary of her calibre going free in the area. Unless and until she decides to leave the job herself, she stays. If you don't like it, I'm afraid you'll just have to put up with it.'

'I don't *have* to put up with anything!' she flashed in swift resentment. 'We're not married yet.'

'True,' came the unmoved agreement. 'You want to back out?'

The offer came like a bolt from the blue, and with as much impact. She lowered her gaze to her plate, swallowing on sudden dryness at the thought of losing him altogether. 'Do you?' she asked unevenly.

'No.' He said it without undue emphasis. 'I'm not the one looking for reasons. I can't force you into marriage, Gina. It has to be your decision, freely made.

'And unconditional!'

'That wasn't a condition, it was an ultimatum,' he rejoined. 'Even if I could respond to it, I wouldn't.'

'On principle, you mean?'

His shrug was lacking in tolerance. 'If you like. You still didn't answer the question. Do you want to back out?'

She shook her head, not quite meeting his gaze, and heard a faint sigh as he settled back in his chair.

'So let's leave it at that, shall we?'

It seemed, Gina thought, that she had no other choice. She would simply have to teach herself to tolerate Fiona and trust Nick to leave her alone.

They watched the display of Scottish dancing for an hour after dinner, then retired to the bar to join a couple who had bought two weeks in one of the luxury apartments upstairs. Dexter and Emma Renniston were around Nick's age and, like themselves, joint partners in business—copying machines and the ilk, in their case.

Made redundant five years before, Dex, as he preferred to be called, had used his contacts to set up in competition with the company that had dispensed with his services. Fair-haired, and sure of his own masculine appeal, he reminded Gina too much of Paul for comfort. Emma was different altogether, although by no means self-effacing. They had owned space at Langhill since the first year of its inception.

'We bought a couple of July weeks in Spain too,' Emma admitted when she and Gina were chatting together while the two men discussed cars. 'We plan on alternating them each year, and using the others for exchange.' She gave Gina a speculative glance. 'Are you and Nick just business partners, or something more?'

Gina smiled and lifted her shoulders. 'I suppose it would have to be something more.'

'He's a piece older than you, isn't he?'

'Not that much.'

'I'd have said at least ten years. Not that that's a bad thing.' Her smile held a certain wry quality. 'I'm a year older than Dex. Sometimes that feels more like ten! Men mature far more slowly.'

Gina said diffidently, 'He seems mature enough to me.'

The older woman laughed. 'Not like your Nick. Now there's an exception to the rule! A man any woman could rely on.'

For what? came the thought, hastily quelled. No more of that, Gina told herself firmly. Tolerance and trust: those were the things she had to work on.

The four of them parted at eleven. Heading for the second-floor stairs with Nick, Gina found herself wishing they were already married and able to retire to the privacy of their very own apartment the way the Rennistons were doing. Having Nick come to her room to spend the night was hardly the same.

'I didn't get to see the apartment you're proposing we use yet,' she said. 'Is it too late to take a look now?'

'Of course not,' he said. 'I didn't realise.' He turned back the way they had come, passing the Rennistons' door to take a corridor at right angles. 'It's at the rear of the house, overlooking the gardens. Not quite as large as the other two, but we don't need three bedrooms.'

'You don't need a key to get in?' she asked as he came to a halt at another of the imposing mahogany doors.

'It isn't locked,' he acknowledged. 'So far it's only furnished with the larger pieces. Unlikely anyone is going to walk away with those.'

Before ushering her inside, he reached in and depressed a wall switch, flooding the spacious living area with soft lamplight. Carpeted in dusky pink, with furnishings in graceful Regency style, the whole room was designed to suit the ambience of the house. Pink-and-gold-striped silk drapes, undrawn at present, framed french doors giving access to a balcony which would get the sun almost the whole day.

A smaller but more than adequate dining area was reached via an archway, in turn giving access to a well-equipped kitchen in natural wood. Through another door was a short corridor off which lay the two bedrooms, one with double bed, the other containing matching singles. A quite superb bathroom completed the lay-out.

'Will it do?' asked Nick from the doorway of the latter as Gina tried out the gold-plated taps. 'As a temporary measure, I mean.'

'It's fantastic!' she responded with genuine enthusiasm. 'Couldn't be better!' She turned as a thought struck her, heart contracting to see him standing there, one hand resting lightly on the jamb. 'But what about the loss in revenue?'

'It will only be this year, at the most,' he said. 'We can start selling subsequent years. This place isn't geared to long-term occupation, anyway.'

'Especially if we start a family.' The comment was out before she could stop it—without even thinking about it—eliciting a sudden stillness on Nick's part.

'Is that what you want?'

It was difficult to tell what his reaction really was. Gina made some attempt to laugh the moment off. 'I suppose it's always a possibility. Particularly as...' Her voice trailed away as realisation struck home. More than a possibility. How could she have been so dumb?

'Particularly as we neither of us took precautions against the event,' Nick finished for her evenly. 'At least, I'm assuming you didn't...don't?'

Her head came up. 'No.'

'Then I'd say it's a distinct probability.' He studied her face, still revealing little of his own inner thoughts. 'Something we'll have to deal with if and when.'

But not something he himself would be overjoyed about, Gina surmised, and felt a sinking sensation deep down inside. It had already happened; she knew that with a certainty she couldn't have explained to anyone. Premonition, presentiment—call it whatever. She knew!

She kept her expression under strict control. 'We could start as of now, if you like. Obviously we'd have to wait until I could see a doctor.' She paused. 'Unless you...?'

Nick shook his head, smile dry. 'No, I haven't. A bit like shutting the stable door after the horse has bolted, in any case. If it happens, it happens. We'll deal with it.' He added abruptly. 'Have you seen enough?'

'To be going on with,' she said. 'There's quite a lot still needs doing to make the place habitable.'

He stood away from the door to allow her exit from the room, making no attempt to touch her as she passed. 'All in hand. By this time next week, it will be fully equipped.'

By this time next week they would be within twenty-four hours of tying the knot, she thought. Less time than that had passed since Nick had come to her in the night, so how could she possibly know she was pregnant with his child?

Wishful thinking, perhaps? A desire to cement the relationship once and for all? Only he didn't really want a child. He had made that pretty clear. Instead of bringing them closer together it might well drive them apart. She had to cling to the hope that she was wrong.

There was no difference in the way he kissed her at her bedroom door. If she left things there, she realised, the pattern would be much the same as the previous night. Much as she longed for his lovemaking, she had to have time to make the necessary arrangements. Too late it might well be, but she could at least try.

'We neither of us got much sleep last night,' she said haltingly. 'And you have a judo class in the morning. Would you mind if we called it a night as of now?'

The landing lighting was good enough to show the sudden ironing out of all expression from the lean features. 'Might not be a bad idea,' he granted. 'See you at breakfast, then.'

If she felt like eating at all, Gina reflected. Safe in her room, with the door closed against him, she resisted the urge to open it again and call him back. Better this way. She could indulge herself to the full again tomorrow night when all was taken care of. No point in worrying about something still to be proven.

Nick had eaten and left by the time she did get down to the dining-room after oversleeping by more than an hour. Mental exhaustion was the only possible cause she could come up with. It certainly wasn't a normal occurrence.

The doctor with whom she had registered at Nick's instigation held surgery from eight-thirty until ten. She would have to borrow one of the company vehicles in order to get there in time. No appointments system, thank heaven. She might have had to wait days before she could be fitted in on a supposedly non-urgent matter.

She arrived at the surgery at nine-fifteen to find several people still waiting. By the time her turn came round she was aware that she wasn't going to make it back to Langhill by ten for her class. Rob would have to keep the dozen or so pupils happy until she arrived, Gina decided resignedly. Not ideal, but it couldn't be helped. For now, this was more important.

The doctor was elderly and taciturn with it. He didn't even look at her as she made her request.

'I didn't get your records through yet,' he said when she finished. 'I can't be prescribing anything of that nature until I've seen them.'

'There'll be nothing there,' Gina protested. 'I can't even remember the last time I had to visit a doctor!'

'Best to be sure,' came the dour response. 'If you make an appointment with my receptionist on your way out, I'll check you over first myself.'

'Can't you do that now?' she asked desperately. 'I'm getting married next week.'

There was no softening of attitude. 'Then you should have thought about it earlier. In any case, with some types of Pill you would have to use additional forms of contraception during the first two weeks of taking it while the system adjusts. Your husband-to-be will have to accept some responsibility. Who is he?'

Gina stood up. 'I don't think that matters very much. Thank you, Doctor.'

She didn't bother making the appointment. There seemed little point in it. Nick might well have agreed to accepting responsibility if they hadn't already put the cart before the horse. Whether he would still, she wasn't sure. Considering what he had said last night, it seemed doubtful. Yet if he genuinely didn't want lumbering with a child...

She was going around in circles and getting nowhere, came the wry acknowledgement. If she was pregnant, Nick himself was more to blame than she was, for taking too much for granted. She could only hope he would appreciate that fact.

It was gone ten-thirty when she finally made it to the gym. Most of her class had departed, the few remaining members none too pleased over being kept waiting. Gina couldn't blame them. They had paid a fee entitling them to five half-hour sessions, and would have organised other commitments around the given times. She would have to offer the ones who had missed out a choice of refund or an extra session, whichever was required.

Rob was keeping an eye on a couple of over-enthusiastic fifty-year-olds using the apparatus when she went back to the main gym.

'Probably the first time they've attempted this in years,' he said. 'I'm going to call a halt in a couple of minutes before one of them has a heart attack!' He added, 'Nick was looking for you a while back.'

'Then I'd better go and find out what he wants,' she returned. 'After I have a shower, that is.'

Her hair felt sticky with perspiration. She washed it while she was under the shower, and left it loose down her back to dry. Her face in the make-up mirror looked different. There was a faint puffiness under her eyes and some lines at the corners which she was sure hadn't been there before. Just twenty-three, and already starting to deteriorate, she thought depressedly. And how would she look in a few months if maybe became certainty? Would Nick still want her when she was fat and ugly?

He was coming along the glass-walled corridor as she started back. He stopped to wait for her, gaze moving over the moisture-slicked fall of her hair before coming to rest on her face. 'What happened to you?' he asked.

'I've been in the shower,' she said, and saw his mouth take on a slant.

'I can see that. I meant before. You were missing more than an hour.'

The truth was too bald, she decided. Hardly a subject to be discussed in a public corridor, at any rate. 'I went for a run. It's allowed isn't it?'

Grey eyes narrowed. 'Why so defensive? It was a reasonable question.'

'More like an inquisition,' she shot back. 'I don't ask you where you've been every time you're out of sight!'

'I don't leave people hanging around the way you did this morning. Being a partner in the business doesn't give you *carte blanche* to run out on your responsibilities whenever the mood happens to take you! You set the time for your class; the least you can do is be there to take it.'

'The same way you're there to take yours?' Gina enquired with silky inflection. 'It is Thursday, isn't it?'

'The judo session was cancelled through lack of comers.' Nick's voice had a clipped quietness more telling than if he had shouted. 'I'm not sure what this is about, but I'm going to find out!' He took her arm in a vice-like grip, turning her about. 'We'll go for a walk.'

There was a side-entrance to the corridor, giving access to the gardens. He took her out into the sunshine, only releasing her when they were away from the door.

'So, let's have it,' he commanded. 'From the top. I realised there was something wrong last night, but it wasn't the time to start pushing.'

'There's nothing wrong,' Gina denied. 'I told you, I went for a run. I forgot the time, that's all.'

'Rubbish!' he came back forcefully. 'You're lying through your teeth.'

'No,' she said.

He stopped in his tracks to take both her shoulders in a grip of iron and force her to look at him. 'Tell me!'

The fight went out of her suddenly. What was the use of trying to hide anything from him? 'I went to see the doctor,' she admitted. 'It took longer than I allowed for.'

His brows had drawn together. 'If it was for the reason I'm thinking, it might still be too late.'

'I know,' she agreed, 'but I had to try.'

'You got what you went for?'

Gina shook her head. 'He wouldn't write me a prescription without making sure I don't have any physical disorders.'

'Sensible man.' The comment was dry. 'Too many just dish them out regardless.' He took his hands away but made no move to continue the walk. 'So why not accept the situation as it is?'

She dropped her eyes. 'It wouldn't bother you if I were pregnant?'

The reply was just a fraction too long in coming. 'Why should it? Most men like the idea of fatherhood.'

In other words, he would adjust where necessary, she thought, the same way he had adjusted to the situation with Paul. There was little enough comfort to be found in that.

'Don't look so gloomy.' His tone had lost its edge. 'There are worse things. This time next week we'll be on the plane and heading for Paris.'

'For a second honeymoon,' Gina responded with a weak attempt at humour. 'I always swore I'd do it the old-fashioned way.'

Nick laughed. 'Not a good idea. Weddings are traumatic enough without first-night nerves added on!' He reached out to touch her hair. 'It's almost dry. I'd better let you go and get changed. I'll be out to lunch,' he added, 'but I should be back in good time for our evening run.'

The 'our' heartened her. He was right. Let it ride. What would be, would be.

CHAPTER ELEVEN

IT WAS only later, when Gina was in her room, that it occurred to her to wonder who Nick was lunching with. A business meeting probably, though to what purpose Gina could only guess. It was high time she began taking an interest in the financial side of things herself, she decided. It was, after all, in her future interests.

She spent the afternoon across at the centre helping Rob organise the following day's swimming gala. It was obvious that Nick hadn't yet mentioned their plans, so she took it on herself to do it.

'We thought we'd ask you and Deirdre to stand witness for us,' she finished. 'Would you mind?'

'*I* wouldn't; I can't speak for Deirdre,' he said. He hesitated before tagging on, 'Why us two in particular? We're not exactly a pair.'

Gina answered with care. 'You seem to get along OK.'

'I suppose we do.' Rob gave her a sideways glance. 'It takes more than that.'

'You mean you're not attracted to her?'

'Yes—no!' He stopped, shaking his head. 'It's not that simple.'

Because he still carried a torch for Fiona, Gina surmised. Not a great deal to be done about that except hope he eventually got over it. There was little chance of his getting anywhere with the woman, even if he made the attempt now that Nick was out of the running. She was out for bigger fish than a mere gym instructor.

'I'll ask Deirdre tonight after class,' she said by way of shelving the subject.

Six o'clock came and went with no sign of Nick. He was still missing when Gina returned from a foreshortened run at seven. Fiona's desk was clear when she went through to the office to see if any messages had been left. A forlorn hope, anyway. Even if Fiona had received one and deliberately neglected to pass it on, she was hardly going to have made a note of it.

The aerobics session went well, with only one drop-out from Tuesday. All good intentions and no stamina, declared Deirdre. She accepted news of the coming wedding with pleasure, and readily acknowledged envy.

'I'm desperate to get married myself,' she confessed. 'I know we're not supposed to be in this day and age, but I can't think of anything better. Always providing the man is right, of course.'

'Anyone in particular in mind?' asked Gina casually, and saw the other girl's colour rise.

'You must have guessed how I feel about Rob. Wasn't that why you put us together on Tuesday?'

Gina smiled and shrugged. 'Just a notion that the two of you might hit it off. How long have you felt that way about him?'

'Oh, ages. He never took too much notice of me before.' She gave a rueful little sigh. 'Not that it's all that different now. You're so lucky, Gina. So is Nick. You were obviously meant for each other. Bad luck on poor Paul though.'

Gina said softly, 'Fiona, too, I suppose.'

'Well, yes—although I can't help feeling glad she didn't get Nick after all. I never did like her.'

'You think everyone accepted that he was going to marry her eventually?'

'I don't know about everyone, but most, I imagine. Fiona certainly gave that impression.' Deirdre looked at her curiously. 'I shouldn't have thought it really mattered. You're the one he asked. I'd settle for that any time.'

Perhaps not, Gina thought, if you knew the real reason. She was facing the swing doors leading from the cafeteria to the stairs. Nick's entry brought an initial relief followed by sudden flaring anger. He'd been gone nine hours. What had she been supposed to think? For all she knew, he could have been lying in some hospital seriously injured—or worse!

Rob was right behind him. The two of them came over to the table where Gina and Deirdre were sitting.

'Living dangerously?' remarked Nick, eyeing the coffee-cups in front of them. 'Either of you like another, or would you prefer something stronger?'

Gina shook her head. 'I'll stick with what I've got, thanks.'

'As you like.' Nick's tone remained easy. 'Deirdre?'

'Not for me either, thanks,' she said with a smile. 'I'm trying to lose weight.'

'You don't need it,' he assured her. He glanced at the younger man standing a little awkwardly by. 'Sit down, Rob; I'll go. Long or short?'

'Lager, please,' returned the other. He hitched out a chair as Nick moved off in the direction of the adjoining bar. 'What happened to the rest of the girls?'

'The last one went home about ten minutes ago,' Deirdre supplied. 'I'll be going myself in a minute.'

'Oh?' The tone was non-committal. 'It seems we're going to be attending a wedding together next week.'

'That's right.' Deirdre had coloured a little.

Gina came to her rescue. 'You both realise no one else is to know, of course? Nick——We don't want any fuss.' She felt bound to offer more explanation than that. 'We neither of us have any family here, you see, so it isn't necessary to go to town on all the trimmings. We prefer to just slip away quietly.'

'You're not planning on keeping it a secret even after the wedding, are you?' asked Rob. 'That might take a bit of doing.'

'More than a bit, I'd say.' Gina shook her head. 'You can let the cat out of the bag as soon as you like once we're gone.'

'Whatever you want. It's your wedding.'

Nick's return with the drinks cut out any reply she might have made. He was wearing a suit, which meant he had come straight over here on return, but that didn't excuse him. Whatever might be lacking in his regard for her, a little thoughtfulness surely wasn't too much to ask?

The wedding wasn't mentioned again. Deirdre made the first move to break up the party after ten minutes or so of desultory conversation.

'I'll see you down to the car,' offered Rob unexpectedly. 'I'm about ready to turn in myself.'

Gina watched the two of them out of the room, hoping her strategy was beginning to pay off. The cafeteria bar had closed, the two staff departed. What customers remained were beginning to drift through to the main bar with its honky-tonk piano and somewhat raucous singing. Catering for all tastes, Nick had said that first day when showing her round. Those who preferred a rather more refined atmosphere stuck to the house facilities.

'I gathered you already asked the two of them to witness,' he said. 'Rob seemed willing enough, if a bit puzzled as to why he'd been accorded the honour. How did Deirdre react?'

'With enthusiasm,' Gina replied expressionlessly. 'She thinks it's all very romantic.'

Nick studied her for a moment, face unrevealing. 'Are you trying to tell me something?'

She clamped down hard on the urge to let fly. 'You might have let me know you were going to be out this long, that's all. I was beginning to think you'd had an accident.'

'Sorry,' he said. 'I got caught up.'

'In what?'

'Business. I went to take another look at that place on the coast I told you about. A rather different concept from Langhill, but with just as great a potential. There's another party interested, so the decision has to be made. It's all set up.'

'And I don't have any say in it, of course.' Gina made no attempt to disguise the acrimony. 'A sleeping partner in every sense!'

A muscle contracted along the strong jawline. 'That's hardly doing either of us justice. Martin was all for expansion. I'm simply carrying on with the plans we'd already made. You won't be losing out.'

Which was true enough, she was bound to admit. One could hardly lose what one had never had to start with. So far as the business itself was concerned, she had no jurisdiction whatsoever until she came into full partnership. Until then she was dependent on Nick for everything.

'Do I still continue drawing a salary after we're married?' she asked abruptly.

'If you continue to work, naturally,' came the answer. 'What you do with it is entirely your affair.' A faint smile touched his lips. 'I shan't be asking for any contribution to household expenses.'

Gina forced herself to lighten up. 'At least I'll be tax deductible!'

'All the way.' Nick finished off his drink and pushed the glass aside. 'Are you ready to go?'

Pulse jerking, she said, softly, 'Where?'

He looked back at her steadily. 'That largely depends on you.'

She didn't want it to depend on her, Gina admitted. She wanted to be swept off her feet—left with no options. Only when Nick was making love to her did she feel any kind of security.

There were plenty of people still around at the house. Only when the last of them had willingly departed were the outer doors closed and locked for the night. Few stayed later than eleven or so in the week.

The Rennistons were part of a small group still chatting over drinks. Dexter waved an arm. 'Come and join us for a nightcap,' he invited.

'Another time, perhaps,' Nick returned easily. 'It's been a heavy day.'

Mounting the stairs at his side, Gina heard a sudden burst of laughter from the same group of people, and suspected it was in response to some suggestive comment of Dexter's concerning the two of them. If Nick thought the same he showed no reaction. Not worth concerning herself over either, she thought.

He kissed her with satisfying thoroughness outside her door, but made no move to come into the room with her. It was left to Gina to say thickly, 'Is this goodnight for us too?'

'Not unless you want it that way,' he said. 'I'll be back after I have a shower and shave. OK?'

She would have settled for him just the way he was, but she couldn't bring herself to betray that degree of need. 'Fine,' she said.

It was less than half an hour until he came, but it seemed more like half the night. Lying in his arms in the pulsing aftermath of their tumultuous love-making, she put aside all stored resentment. She might have no real part in the business as yet, but this was one facet of their relationship in which she played a major role. It would do for now.

Friday brought a telephone call from Paul. Gina took it in the privacy of the sitting-room. He had deliberately held off, he said, to give her time to think things through and realise just how foolish she was being. Surely by now she had come to her senses?

'I didn't change my mind,' she responded, trying to sound positive about it. 'By this time next week I'll be married to Nick.'

'Next week!' Paul sounded dumbfounded. 'Why the rush?'

Gina caught her lower lip between her teeth. She hadn't meant to let it out like that. On the other hand, he was too far away for it to matter very much, she reassured herself.

'It's what we both want,' she said. 'Please try to understand, Paul. I love him.'

'You love *me*,' he insisted. 'At least, you did.'

Never! she wanted to deny, but that would have been too bald and hurtful. 'It's different with Nick,' she said instead.

'You mean he made it to first base?' There was bitter irony in the remark. 'You never gave me the chance to prove what I could do in that department.' His tone altered. 'I'd take a bet he's planning on landing you with a baby at first opportunity, so that you'll have something to occupy you other than the business—and whatever else he might get up to. You can guarantee you'll not be the only woman in his life!'

'Nothing is guaranteed,' she returned tonelessly. 'Please don't contact me again, Paul. It won't change anything.'

She replaced the receiver with an unsteady hand, and sat for a moment gathering herself together. There was every possibility that, while not particularly eager to become a father, Nick did indeed see a child as a means to an end. That would explain his whole attitude to the subject. But it didn't mean she had to accept a back-seat role when the time came for her to take an active part in business affairs.

She resolutely kept her mind from dwelling on the other suggestion. Infidelity was a risk factor in any relationship. She would just have to hope for the best.

Fiona was at her desk when she went through to the office. Unable to pass by without making some kind of effort, Gina found herself saying tentatively, 'Busy?'

'Very,' came the cool rejoinder. 'The problem with taking a day off.'

Gina paused, aware of a sudden heaviness in her chest. 'You weren't here yesterday?'

The dark head didn't turn. 'No. If you're looking for Nick, he went to Glasgow.'

'Thanks, I already know that.' Gina hadn't, but she wasn't about to admit it. 'I'll leave you to get on, then.'

Once outside the door, she let out her breath on a sigh. The fact that Fiona had been off yesterday was in no way proof that she had accompanied Nick. If the latter had been the truth, the other would have surely been unable to resist the opportunity to let her triumph be known, if not in actual words then in implication.

Unless, of course, he had warned her against betraying any hint.

Circumstantial evidence, nothing more, she concluded resolutely. She was building a mountain out of nothing more substantial than a couple of worm casts.

Nick was back in time to join her on the evening run. A few details to finalise, he acknowledged when she asked what he'd been doing in Glasgow.

'We can start selling on the strength of a prospectus and Langhill's reputation,' he declared as they left the house. 'Six months should see the place ready for occupation. After that, it's a case of building up facilities the way we did here. You're going to be a very wealthy lady.'

Every penny of which she would willingly give in exchange for the one assurance he couldn't yet offer her, thought Gina achingly. Moving at her side, supple as a panther in the all black track-suit, he turned her bones to jelly. What was mere money compared to the feelings he aroused in her?

The weekend brought yet another change-over in clientele, along with a sudden and depressing change in the weather. Gazing out at the driving rain on the Sunday morning, Gina felt sympathy for those newly arrived. The leisure centre was going to be over-populated.

'One thing we can't govern is the climate,' said Nick at breakfast. His eyes took on a glint as he surveyed her across the table. 'We could always go back to bed.'

There might come a day, Gina thought ruefully, when she no longer blushed at the memory of their lovemaking. 'Hardly worthwhile,' she responded, trying to make a joke of it. 'I can't sleep in daylight. How about a game of squash before lunch?'

Nick gave a mock sigh. 'I could think of better ways of working off surplus energy, but you're on. Better reserve a court. I've a feeling they're going to be in short supply today.'

They were. Half an hour at ten-fifteen was all that was left. A glassed-in corridor ran above the courts, from which spectators could watch the games in progress. Gina felt a bit like a fish in a bowl when she and Nick made their entrances under the concerted gazes of several interested viewers.

Nick looked good in shorts, she thought, as he despatched a couple of warm-up services. He had the legs for it. She knew the power in those tanned and muscular thighs. The very recollection sent tremors down her spine.

'Ready?' he asked, turning to look at her, and she hastily wiped out the expression she knew must be in her eyes.

'Ready,' she said.

The match was hard fought. Attention concentrated on the ball, Gina forgot about the watching eyes above. Nick was playing to win, giving her no quarter. It required every ounce of skill she possessed to stay with him.

He won the first game, but she took the second. At fourteen-all in the third, he set the game to three, making it seventeen points to win instead of the normal fifteen. At sixteen-all Gina lost service with a double fault, and conceded defeat with good grace as they had run out of time. They left the court to a smattering of applause from the viewers above.

'How about a coffee upstairs?' suggested Nick. 'I feel in need of a pick-me-up.'

Damp with perspiration, Gina would have liked to have gone straight back to the house to take a shower, but the thought of liquid refreshment after so much effort was tempting.

'What do we do for the rest of the day?' she asked as they made their way to the cafeteria. 'It's still raining cats and dogs.'

'Whatever takes your fancy,' came the amenable reply. 'I'm all yours.'

If only, she thought, she could be wholly sure of that. Loving Nick was one thing, trusting him a whole other ball-game. Only now, with Fiona temporarily out of reach, was there any real sense of security.

The cafeteria was doing good business. Gina secured one of the last remaining tables while Nick went to fetch the coffee. Typically, he made no attempt to pull rank, but joined the line-up for service.

'Slumming with the rank and file?' asked Dexter Renniston, taking one of the spare seats. 'I'd have thought you'd prefer your own quarters to this mêlée!'

Still standing, his wife proffered a faintly apologetic smile. 'All right if we join you?'

Gina rallied herself to smile back. 'Of course. Nick went to get coffee.'

'Why don't you go and do the same, Dex?' Emma said pointedly. 'You could do with the exercise.'

'No rest for the wicked,' he quipped, getting reluctantly to his feet again. 'I was looking forward to an intimate tête-à-tête with our blonde Amazon here while *you* went and got the coffee.'

Emma took a seat herself, shaking her head with an air of resignation as he moved off. 'Don't take it he was joking either! He has a weakness for blondes—especially when they're young and nubile. I knew it when I married him, but I thought he'd grow out of it. Just goes to show what fools women are when it comes to men. They don't change.' She paused, expression undergoing a subtle alteration. 'Talking of which, we spotted Nick in Oban yesterday with that secretary of his—Fiona, isn't it?'

'That's right.' Gina was surprised by the steadiness of her voice. 'They were there on business.'

'Oh?' For a moment the other looked nonplussed. She rallied with a laugh and a shrug. 'Nothing to worry about, then. As I said last night, you're lucky. If it had been Dex, now...'

Gina made no attempt to take her up on the invitation implicit in the pause. Whatever problems the Renniston marriage might be facing, she had no interest in hearing about them. Nine hours Nick had been gone on Thursday, and all of them spent with Fiona. Oh, he'd no doubt fitted business in too, but the other woman had been right there with him.

Oban. She hadn't even known that much. Somewhere on the coast was all he had told her.

'I think I'm going to have to go for a shower,' she said, suddenly uncaring of whether or not Emma guessed the truth. 'I'm too hot and sticky to wait.' She was gathering up her racquet bag as she spoke, pushing back the chair to rise jerkily to her feet. 'See you later, maybe.'

The rain hammered against the glass as she went along the connecting corridor to the house. There wasn't much chance of its clearing at all today, according to the forecast, although tomorrow promised to be brighter. Gina wished she could say the same about her state of mind.

It had been a probability all along, of course, but confirmation was still a shock. How Nick had managed to talk the Scottish woman into continuing their association she didn't care to dwell on too deeply. She knew just how persuasive he could be.

What she was going to do about it now that she did know she wasn't yet sure. How could she marry a man who not only didn't love her, but was carrying on with other women even before the marriage took place? How could she give him up when the thought alone made her want to curl up and die?

The shower refreshed her body but went no way towards easing the mental anguish. Emerging into the bedroom to find Nick waiting for her made matters no easier. She wasn't ready for confrontation.

'Are you OK?' he asked, scanning her face. 'Emma thought you might be feeling ill, you left so suddenly.'

'I felt too sticky to hang on,' Gina answered expressionlessly. 'Sorry about the coffee.'

'It isn't important.' A frown creased the space between his brows. 'Are you sure you're all right? You look a bit pale.'

The towel that was her only covering was slipping. She clutched it more securely about her. 'I'm fine. I'd be even better for a little privacy while I dress.'

His smile came low and teasing. 'I've seen you in less.'

'Not in daylight.' She was fighting to retain control of the emotions threatening to choke her. 'I mean it, Nick. I want you to go. You'd no right to just walk in here in the first place.'

The lean features went suddenly taut. 'If that's the way you feel, I'll leave you to get on with it.'

Say something, an inner voice urged her as he turned on his heel, but the words remained stuck in her throat. The closing of the door between them was like an omen.

CHAPTER TWELVE

THE rain turned to drizzle and finally petered out altogether around two o'clock. Gazing out from the window at the drenched landscape, Gina thought it looked almost as wretched as she felt.

Missing lunch had been no hardship because she couldn't have eaten a thing, but she could hardly spend the rest of the day hiding away up here. The decision she had come to after so much soul-searching had to be put into practice.

She found Nick running some figures through the computer in the office. He looked at her with veiled eyes as she hesitated just inside the door.

'Something you wanted to say?' he asked.

The total unemotionalism cleared away any remaining reservations. She slipped the sapphire ring from her finger, and stepped forward to place it on the desk. 'It's over, Nick. I changed my mind.'

He made no attempt to pick the ring up, or even to look at it, but just continued to regard her with that same lack of expression.

'Why now?' he asked. 'You were fine up to my going for the coffee.' His eyes narrowed fractionally. 'Does Emma Renniston have anything to do with all this?'

The moment of accusation came and went. He would have some plausible excuse all ready and waiting, Gina told herself. 'Only obliquely,' she said. 'I looked at her and Dex, and suddenly saw the two of us in a few years time.'

Dark brows drew together. 'There's no comparison.'

'There's no depth of feeling between them,' she stated flatly. 'Any more than there is between us. I must have been crazy to ever let things get this far!'

Nick got up to go and close the door she had left standing ajar, turning with his back to it to give her a long and penetrating scrutiny.

'Crazy or not, you're stuck with it,' he said.

'How?' she challenged. 'You can't force me to marry you!'

'Nature might supply the coercion. The chances have multiplied, wouldn't you say?'

A wave of dismay swept through her. She had totally forgotten about that. She rallied with an effort. 'My own problem.'

'Not,' he came back hardily, 'if you're carrying *my* child. The father has rights too.'

'It's a possibility, not a certainty.'

'A probability,' he corrected, 'until proven otherwise.'

He was right, she thought, remembering her conviction. A probability indeed!

'There are plenty of babies born outside marriage,' she said.

'Not mine.' He paused, shaking his head in sudden rejection. 'This is ridiculous!'

'It was ridiculous to think it might work in the first place,' Gina defended. She drew in a breath, becoming aware of the trembling of her limbs. 'I want to go back home.'

'You don't have one to go to any more,' he pointed out.

'So I'll find somewhere else to live. If I can't get my old job back, I'll find another of those too.' She was too desolate to care about the final detail. 'I've enough money put by to tide me over for a few weeks, so you won't need to make any concessions. You can buy me out at the end of the two years, as you first suggested. That way, we'll both be happy.'

For a long moment he just stood there looking at her, face carved from stone. When he spoke it was on a cool hard note. 'When did you plan on leaving?'

Her chin lifted. 'Will tomorrow be soon enough?'

'Don't read meanings that aren't there,' he clipped. 'What about your other commitments? You don't mind walking out on those?'

'Rob can cope.'

'Not with aerobics. The very least you can do is finish out the week already signed up.'

He was right, she knew. She had a duty to the people expecting a certain service for their money. Rob and Deirdre would have to know that the wedding was off, of course, though what explanation she was going to give she couldn't begin to imagine as yet.

'The...arrangements,' she said haltingly. 'You'll see to things?'

'Yes.' Nick moved away from the door, back to his seat at the console. 'If that's it,' he said over a shoulder, 'I have work to do.'

Which was as much as she really meant to him, Gina thought painfully, turning to go. All he had ever cared about was the business. Well, he could have it: lock, stock and barrel!

She spent most of the afternoon working out across at the gym. As if sensing her need to be alone, Rob made no effort to approach her. He went off for the day at four.

Tomorrow, Gina promised herself, she would put him in the picture. Deirdre too, of course. All she had to say was that she had changed her mind about marrying Nick, and let them make of it what they would. After the way she had treated Paul, they would probably regard her with disgust, but she couldn't help that. Once this week was over, she wouldn't be seeing anyone here ever again.

It might be an idea to contact the health club where she had worked and ask if they had filled her job yet. There was little chance of being able to afford even a bedsit in Cambridge itself, so that meant looking around the outlying areas, but she had friends down there who would help her out until she was settled again. Not Paul though. That was finished too. If she couldn't have Nick the way she wanted him, she wanted no one.

She made herself get ready and go down for dinner around eight o'clock. Having heard nothing from the room next door since returning from her run, she had assumed that Nick had gone out, and was taken aback to see him already seated at table.

'We need to talk,' he said as she slid reluctantly into her chair. He held up a hand as she made to speak. 'Just hear me out.'

Gina subsided again, feeling the painful contraction about her heart as she looked across at the strong features. Difficult to believe, viewing his remote expression, that he had ever made love to her with such passion.

'Assuming you're still interested in setting up your own club,' he continued, 'if results prove negative, I'll back you.'

'And if it proves positive?' she asked thickly.

'You marry me for the child's sake.' His voice was level, his gaze steady. 'Illegitimacy might not carry the same stigma these days, but it's hardly fair to hang the label if it can be avoided.'

He was putting her in a cleft stick, she thought. Outright refusal would imply that she was thinking only of herself. And yet wasn't that exactly what she was doing? Any child they might have conceived between them would be entitled to its birthright.

Back to square one, she concluded wryly. It was going to be a couple of weeks before she would know one way or the other. Right at this moment, she wasn't sure what she wanted the result to be.

Nick was watching her face, assessing her reactions. 'Well?' he prompted.

'I don't seem to have any choice,' she said on a note of resignation. 'What do we tell Deirdre and Rob?'

He shrugged. 'Just that the wedding has been postponed. What else can we tell them?'

What else indeed? Gina thought bleakly.

She left him as soon as they had finished dinner, to spend a lonely evening and an even lonelier night. Tossing and turning into the small hours, she wondered if Nick might be missing her too. She even found herself hoping she *was* pregnant, so that she had a face-saving excuse to backtrack on her decision. Fiona or no Fiona, she loved him still.

*   *   *

With the weather failing to improve a great deal, the leisure facilities drew maximum usage over the following couple of days. Gina spent most of her time there.

She waited until the Tuesday to tell Rob about the postponement, anticipating his confusion.

'We decided to let it ride for a while,' she finished lamely. 'You know the old saying "Marry in haste et cetera".'

'I could have quoted you that one last week,' he said. 'It strikes me you don't really know who you want, Gina. Nick...' he hesitated, obviously reluctant to say it '...well, he's not exactly your age-group, is he? Eleven years is a big gap between husband and wife.'

I wouldn't care if it were twenty years, she wanted to respond, but she held it back. There was no point in confusing him even more.

Deirdre's reaction to the news was one of pure disappointment.

'I was really looking forward to it,' she confessed. 'Still, it was a bit soon, I suppose. Was it your decision to wait a while, or Nick's?'

'Mutual,' Gina lied. 'We both got carried away.'

The other girl's smile was wry. 'I wish Rob would get carried away!'

Unlikely, Gina reflected. Not while Fiona was still around.

The Scottish woman was just leaving for the day when Gina went across at five-thirty to change for her evening run. Meeting the cool glance, Gina wondered how much, if anything, Nick had told her. If it turned out that a shotgun wedding was after all unnecessary, the other could hope again.

Whether that hope would eventually be fulfilled was something else entirely.

Nick himself was talking with some people in the hall. Gina passed the group without pausing, to run lightly up the stairs. From the way he was dressed, she guessed he was planning on going out. Maybe even to pick Fiona up after giving her time to change her clothing. Two nights of celibacy must be taking their toll.

The remedy was in her own hands, of course. All she had to do was tell him she would marry him regardless. She would be no worse off than she had been before. Almost anything had to be better, she thought, than this aching emptiness.

At ten-thirty, when she eventually retired for the night, he still hadn't returned. Preparing for bed, Gina fought a brief and losing battle. Where was the point in waiting another week to discover what every instinct in her already knew was so? Where was the point in denying her love for Nick simply because his feelings didn't run as deep? If Fiona had ever really meant anything to him, he would have done something about it long before she herself arrived on the scene. She could oust her altogether if she really put her mind to it.

The room next door wasn't locked. Gina slid inside like a wraith, without switching on any lights. The bed was already pulled out, she saw, as her eyes adjusted to the darkness.

She was between the sheets though far from sleep when Nick eventually returned some unknown time later.

'Don't put the light on,' she said as soon as he opened the door.

He stood still for an endless moment, gazing across to where she lay. When he did speak he sounded constrained. 'Is this some kind of game you're playing?'

'No game,' Gina assured him huskily. 'I want you, Nick.'

He still didn't move. 'Regardless of consequences?'

'As you said, it's probably too late, anyway.' She was doing her best to stay in control. 'I finally got my priorities sorted out.'

'And this, I take it, is one of them?' There was irony in his voice. 'Nice to know I didn't lose my touch after all.' He closed the door quietly, sliding out of his jacket as he came over to where she lay. 'No more mind-changing,' he stated.

He shed the rest of his clothing without undue haste. Gina watched him with fast-beating heart, loving the fine clean lines of his body, the ripple of muscle across powerful shoulders. Every inch of him the pure, masculine male.

Kneeling on the mattress edge, he drew the sheet slowly down the length of her body, allowing a finger to trail lightly over her skin in its wake. She trembled to his touch, surrendering herself to sensation as he found the moist centre of her being.

His hand was so sure yet so sensitive, knowing just where and just how, tearing moans of sheer pleasure from her throat. She moved her body wantonly, every sense in her tuned to the silky caress.

Lowering himself, he put his mouth to hers. The kiss started slow and gentle, teasing her lips apart to taste the inner sweetness, deepening to passion as she responded in kind.

She played her fingers over his back, followed the curve of his spine to the deep cleft of his buttocks, and felt the firm male hemispheres tense beneath her exploring hands. His hips were narrow, the flesh taut. She heard his breath drawn in sharply as she curved her hand to the pulsing heat of his manhood, cherishing the shape of him, the power of him: steel wrapped in velvet, vibrant with life.

Nick said her name on a shaken breath as she took him to her. He entered her smoothly, deeply, pausing for the space of a single heartbeat before starting to move with ever-increasing hunger. Limbs wrapped about him, she matched each fevered thrust, exulting in the fierceness of his possession. How could she ever have considered leaving him? He was life itself to her!

Fulfilment came with shattering force, followed bare seconds later by Nick's hoarse cry. She cradled the proud dark head on her breast, content for the moment just to have him near. Tomorrow would be time enough to start thinking rationally again. For tonight, she could let herself believe he loved her as she loved him.

'No more doubts?' he murmured against her skin some time later.

About to confirm, Gina hesitated. Why lie about it? 'You took Fiona with you to Oban last week,' she said softly.

He lifted his head to look at her, expression concealed by the darkness. 'Who told you?'

'The Rennistons saw you together.'

His breath came out on a sudden sigh. 'It wasn't what you think. I'd fixed up an interview for her that same afternoon. It seemed the least I could do was to take her in and introduce her. We had dinner together afterwards, but that was as far as it went. She starts next week.'

A cautious relief was beginning to spread through her. 'Based in Oban?'

'Based wherever Larry happens to be at any given time. He's a financier. He travels all over the world. He had urgent need of a personal assistant who could also perform the duties of hostess when required. Fiona fitted the bill perfectly.'

'Was it her idea that she leave, or yours?' Gina asked tentatively.

'Hers. I already told you I had my hands tied. The job with Larry just happened to crop up at the right time.'

'You could have told me all that before,' she said.

'I could,' he agreed. 'I just didn't think you'd be too appreciative.' He dropped a light kiss on the tip of her nose. 'Can we forget about Fiona? She'll be gone in a couple of days.'

Gone, perhaps, but *not* forgotten, Gina was sure. She said, 'You'll need someone to take her place.'

'Deirdre's capable enough, if she fancies the job. Otherwise, I'll have to advertise.'

His lips were at her ear, tongue a delicate probe. Her senses were stirring again, the delicious tension spreading through her. He hadn't yet told her where he had been tonight, but that could wait. For now she would settle for this.

Thursday brought a pang in the knowledge that this would have been her wedding-day if she hadn't messed things up. Nick had said nothing so far about setting another date. It was probable, Gina thought, that he was waiting for her to make the move. She was only thankful that she had decided not to tell her mother the news prior to the event.

Fiona left Langhill for good that day too. What passed between her and Nick by way of farewell Gina had no way of knowing and refused to think about it. It was just the two of them now; whether they would eventually prove to be three was still a matter for conjecture. Either way, they would be together.

The call from the solicitor dealing with probate on her father's estate came through on the Friday morning. There were papers requiring signatures from them both before everything could be finalised, he said.

'If we're going into Stirling this afternoon,' said Nick casually over lunch, 'how about booking another date for the wedding? Or would you prefer to do it in more leisurely fashion this time?'

Gina gave herself no time to even think about it. The wedding itself was merely a formality; she was already committed heart and soul. 'As soon as you like,' she said.

His smile was dry. 'Depends on how soon we can be fitted in.'

'Well, whenever, then.' Looking across at him, she yearned for it to be all over and done with. As Nick's wife in name she might begin to feel a certain security of tenure.

Seated in the office where it had all started, she listened with only half an ear while the solicitor went through the basic detail once more. A bare five weeks ago they had occupied these same seats as total strangers. It scarcely seemed possible that so much could have happened in so short a time.

Nick was wearing the same grey suit he had worn that day; the difference being that she now knew every inch of the lean fit body beneath it. The instant and vital attraction that had caused her to harden herself against him still caught her by the throat. That other women would continue to feel that same pull, she was only too well aware. Even with Fiona gone, there would always be someone around to worry about. Without love to sustain it, his desire for her would eventually fade.

'So on your twenty-fifth birthday the financial benefits of your interest in the business become yours to control as you see fit,' intoned the solicitor, drawing her attention back to the present. 'Of course, this gives you no automatic part in the management, but neither does it entail any liability for debts which might be incurred. You——'

'I'm sorry?' Gina came suddenly alive to what the man was saying. 'I'm not sure I understand.'

'It's quite straightforward,' he said. 'A partner in business may assign his interest to anyone he wishes—unless the partnership agreement itself expressly forbids it—but the assignment doesn't make the assignee a partner unless the other partners agree. In this particular case, of course, the onus would be on Mr Calway alone to make that decision.' The last with a brief glance in the younger man's direction. 'A matter to be discussed at some later date, perhaps.'

'Nothing wrong with now,' Nick returned levelly. 'It will be a full working partnership.'

Gina sat motionless, her mind in turmoil. If Nick had already been aware of the facts just outlined, nothing made any sense. Why the concern over her proposed marriage to Paul when the law allowed her no right of interference anyway? All he would have had to do was say the word.

He couldn't have known, she concluded. His whole reason for marrying her himself was based on the need to keep outsiders from gaining any kind of foothold. There had been no cause for him to go to the lengths he had.

She signed what she was asked to sign without further question, too numb to care overmuch. Today, Nick had managed to find a parking space right outside the building. They were in the car again and heading down the hill into town before she could bring herself to speak her mind.

'That,' she said tonelessly, 'must have been as big a shock to you as it was to me.'

Nick gave her a swift glance. 'What exactly are we talking about?'

'The fact that it wouldn't have mattered whether I'd married Paul or not. I mean, if you'd known you held the power of veto all the way, you needn't have done what you did.'

There was a side-turning coming up on the left. Nick indicated and swung into it, bringing the car to a halt at the curbside a couple of dozen yards along the quiet back-street.

'What makes you think I didn't know?' he asked.

Gina's head jerked round, her eyes searching the lean features. 'You . . . can't have.'

His smile was faint. 'You don't enter into any kind of business deal without taking account of eventualities. I'd no more intention of laying myself open to outside influences than Martin had. One of the reasons we opted for a straight partnership instead of forming a company.'

'But then why didn't you just say?' she queried huskily. 'Why go to all that trouble to keep me from marrying Paul?'

The smile came again, accompanied this time by a resigned shrug. 'I'd have thought that was obvious. I was hooked that very first day. The only reason I made the offer to back you after a year was to get you up here. I planned on spending those twelve months in our getting to know one another, only friend Paul scotched that idea. I knew you were physically attracted, so I worked that angle instead. I was ready to do whatever was necessary to stop you from marrying him.'

Gina gazed at him with luminous eyes, feeling the doubt and despondency of the past days ebbing away before a surging tide of pure happiness. He hadn't said the actual word as yet, but he could mean nothing else.

'Why didn't you tell me how you really felt?' she whispered. 'I thought you only...'

'Wanted you for your body?' he supplied as her voice petered out. He put up a hand to caress her cheek, fingers gentle. 'That too, of course. The judo session nearly finished me. I'd never wanted a woman as much as I wanted you that morning. Only it wasn't the time or place. It was Paul himself who precipitated things. Even then I fought shy of laying it all on the line. An in-built defence mechanism, I guess.'

Gina said softly, 'I'd never have married him anyway.'

'I didn't know that at the time. I had to lay claim the only way I could.' Grey eyes took on a luminosity of their own as he looked at her. 'Was it only because of Fiona that you tried to back out of marrying me?'

'Yes,' she admitted. 'But despite her that I came back.'

'Not just the possibility that you might be pregnant?'

'No.' Her smile was tremulous. 'I love you, Nick. I think it happened almost right away, only I thought you were involved with Fiona.'

He drew her to him and kissed her with the tenderness she had yearned for, holding her close as if he would never let her go. 'She means nothing to me,' he murmured against her hair. 'She never did. I broke a golden rule in asking her out to start with, then found myself landed, but I didn't sleep with her.'

She believed him. All the same, she was glad the woman had gone. Clinging to him, she said tentatively, 'Shall you mind too much if I do turn out to be pregnant?'

His laugh came low. 'If I'd minded I'd have made sure it didn't happen—for a while, at least. I suppose I thought a baby might bring us closer.' He held her away from him to search her face. 'How do you feel about it?'

'Hopeful,' she admitted. 'But only because it would be yours, Nick.'

His gaze kindled again. 'Ours,' he corrected. 'Yours and mine both.' He kissed her again, passionately this time. 'Oh, God,' he said thickly, 'I love you!'

'Where are we going?' she asked when he released her and restarted the engine.

'To arrange a wedding,' he said. 'And this time it won't be called off.'

Harlequin is proud to present our best authors, their best books and the best for your reading pleasure!

Throughout 1993, Harlequin will bring you exciting books by some of the top names in contemporary romance!

In February, look for *Twist of Fate* by

JAYNE ANN KRENTZ

Hannah Jessett had been content with her quiet life. Suddenly she was the center of a corporate battle with wealthy entrepreneur Gideon Cage. Now Hannah must choose between the fame and money an inheritance has brought or a love that may not be as it appears.

Don't miss **TWIST OF FATE** ...
wherever Harlequin books are sold.

ROMANCE IS A YEARLONG EVENT!

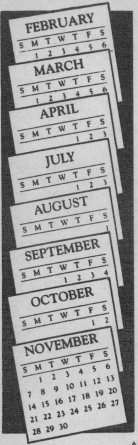

Celebrate the most romantic day of the year with MY VALENTINE! (February)

CRYSTAL CREEK
When you come for a visit Texas-style, you won't want to leave! (March)

Celebrate the joy, excitement and adjustment that comes with being JUST MARRIED! (April)

Go back in time and discover the West as it was meant to be . . . UNTAMED— Maverick Hearts! (July)

LINGERING SHADOWS
New York Times bestselling author Penny Jordan brings you her latest blockbuster. Don't miss it! (August)

BACK BY POPULAR DEMAND!!!
Calloway Corners, involving stories of four sisters coping with family, business and romance! (September)

FRIENDS, FAMILIES, LOVERS
Join us for these heartwarming love stories that evoke memories of family and friends. (October)

Capture the magic and romance of Christmas past with HARLEQUIN HISTORICAL CHRISTMAS STORIES! (November)

WATCH FOR FURTHER DETAILS IN ALL HARLEQUIN BOOKS!

CALEND

Where do you find hot Texas nights, smooth Texas charm and dangerously sexy cowboys?

DEEP IN THE HEART

Wedding Bells—Texas Style!

Even a Boston blue blood needs a Texas education. Ranch owner J. T. McKinney is handsome, strong, opinionated and totally charming. And he is determined to marry beautiful Bostonian Cynthia Page. However, the couple soon discovers a Texas cattleman's idea of marriage differs greatly from a New England career woman's!

CRYSTAL CREEK reverberates with the exciting rhythm of Texas. Each story features the rugged individuals who live and love in the Lone Star State. And each one ends with the same invitation...

Y'ALL COME BACK...REAL SOON!

Don't miss *DEEP IN THE HEART* by Barbara Kaye. Available in March wherever Harlequin books are sold.

HARLEQUIN®

my Valentine

1993

The most romantic day of the year is here! Escape into the exquisite world of love with MY VALENTINE 1993. What better way to celebrate Valentine's Day than with this very romantic, sensuous collection of four original short stories, written by some of Harlequin's most popular authors.

**ANNE STUART
JUDITH ARNOLD
ANNE McALLISTER
LINDA RANDALL WISDOM**

**THIS VALENTINE'S DAY, DISCOVER ROMANCE
WITH MY VALENTINE 1993**

Available in February wherever Harlequin Books are sold.   VAL93